"You just met me three days ago," Mitch said. "How could you be 'captivated' by me?"

Kate blinked back tears. "Because you've done it all right. You accepted responsibility and you found the courage to give your girls every bit of your life and your love. You're a *real* parent. And that's what I so wish I could be."

"You want to be a mother," he said softly, as though he understood.

But he didn't. "I had a daughter," she said, "nearly four years ago. She's—" she blinked through more tears "—the same age as Dee."

"You had a daughter?" he asked, his voice tender with emotion. "What happened, Kate?"

"I gave her up." Her chin trembled, and a sucking gasp escaped.

Her sobs tore through the stillness of the night, but they were soon smothered against the broad planes of Mitch's chest, because he pulled her close, holding her through the pain, through the tears, and whispering the words he must've thought she wanted to hear.

"I'm so sorry, Kate."

But he had no idea who she really was.

Books by Renee Andrews

Love Inspired

Her Valentine Family
Healing Autumn's Heart
Picture Perfect Family
Love Reunited
Heart of a Rancher
Bride Wanted
Yuletide Twins
Mommy Wanted

RENEE ANDREWS

spends a lot of time in the gym. No, she isn't working out. Her husband, a former all-American gymnast, co-owns ACE Cheer Company, an all-star cheerleading company. She is thankful the talented kids at the gym don't have a problem when she brings her laptop and writes while they sweat. When she isn't writing, she's typically traveling with her husband, bragging about their two sons or spoiling their bulldog.

Renee is a kidney donor and actively supports organ donation. She welcomes prayer requests and loves to hear from readers. Write to her at Renee@ReneeAndrews.com, visit her website at www.reneeandrews.com or check her out on Facebook or Twitter.

Mommy Wanted

Renee Andrews

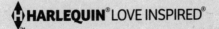
HARLEQUIN® LOVE INSPIRED®

Recycling programs for this product may not exist in your area.

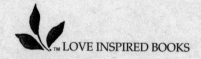

.™ LOVE INSPIRED BOOKS

ISBN-13: 978-0-373-81748-1

MOMMY WANTED

Copyright © 2014 by Renee Andrews

This edition published by arrangement with Love Inspired Books.

® and TM are trademarks of Love Inspired Books, used under license. Trademarks indicated with ® are registered in the United States Patent and Trademark Office, the Canadian Trade Marks Office and in other countries.

www.Harlequin.com

Printed in U.S.A.

Be kind and compassionate to one another, forgiving each other, just as in Christ God forgave you.
—*Ephesians* 4:32

This novel is dedicated to Clair Zeringue,
my amazing mother-in-law. I love you, Mom Z!

Chapter One

Kate Wydell's nervous fingertips rattled the pages of *The Claremont News,* the sound echoing through her car and magnifying her jitters. The Help Wanted section encompassed less than a column, the short list ending with the sole position for which she was qualified. Gillespie Insurance Agency needed an office assistant, no previous insurance experience required. Good people skills, a knowledge of word processing and an ability to remain calm in a crisis were the only criteria for the job.

She had all of those office skills and then some, and over the past year she'd perfected the ability to remain calm during a crisis. Her own personal crisis had led her back to this tiny North Alabama town, a place she'd left behind three years ago without a care in the world… and without regard for her baby girl.

Two blinks and a thick swallow warred against the tears that sought freedom. She would *not* allow herself to cry. Mascara streaks would only showcase the paleness of her face and the cheekbones that seemed much more prominent with the loss of fifteen pounds.

She'd stopped at Hydrangea Park while she gathered her courage and searched the classifieds. Flipping the visor, she checked her makeup in the tiny mirror. She was healthy now; the doctor said so. But did she look sick? Had she used too much blush to compensate for her pallor? Those questions ricocheted through her head, but the biggest and most pressing question now was…

Would Mitch Gillespie recognize her?

She tugged at a rogue black curl dangling precariously near her right eye. The inky corkscrew locks only drew more attention to her ridiculously fair skin. The last time she'd been in Claremont she'd had her trademark tan, an athletic build and blond wavy hair. And the last time she'd been in Claremont, she'd been married to one of Mitch's best friends.

Another look in the mirror. Even her family hadn't recognized her when she'd visited. Why would Mitch?

She took a deep breath, huffed it out. This

would be so much easier if Chad were in town. Then she could tell her ex what she wanted in person and then deal with the consequences of a town that probably still hated her for hurting their golden boy. She hadn't considered that mid-May meant the end of the school year and his break from teaching at the college, when he'd naturally head out of town on vacation. But maybe this was better. She'd get settled in while he was away and have time to prepare for the fireworks when he returned and learned she was back.

God, don't let anyone remember me until I get a chance to talk to Chad.

Praying still felt new for Kate, even though she'd pleaded and begged God aplenty over the past year. Probably enough for a lifetime. And now she'd see if He would truly have mercy on her, and if Chad would have mercy on her, too.

But first she needed a job.

Mitch Gillespie unbuckled Dee's car seat and helped the three-year-old out, while Emmie whimpered from the other side of the car. "I'm coming, sweetie," he said, taking Dee's hand and leading her around the car so he could free her sister.

"Why is her face so red?" Dee asked, peering in as Mitch worked with the abundance of fasteners holding Emmie in place. "'Cause she's sick?" Dee was at an age where she questioned everything, and he tried his best to always provide an answer. "Her eyes look funny, too, like she's sad. Is that 'cause she's sick, too?" she continued.

Mitch's stomach knotted. He hated that his baby was ill, and he hated even more that he had to bring the two of them back to his office because he'd forgotten his laptop. But in the flurry following the call from the day care about Emmie's fever and the need for her to be picked up quickly, he'd forgotten all about the fact that he had several policies that had to be updated today.

"I'm sure it's because of her fever," he said, as Emmie pushed the last strap away and reached tiny hands toward her daddy. Heat radiated from her cheek as Mitch pulled her against him. Eighteen months old, Emmie had experienced a fever only a couple of times, following her immunizations, and she'd never had one due to sickness.

"But you gave her medicine," Dee said, ever the voice of preschooler reason.

"Right, but that was only—" he glanced at his watch "—ten minutes ago. It'll take a little longer for it to kick in."

Dee's strawberry brows furrowed and she frowned. "Everybody's sick. I don't like it when everybody's sick. There's nobody to play with."

Carrying Emmie, Mitch led Dee toward the front door of Gillespie Insurance. Based on what Emmie's teacher said, Dee's statement wasn't that far off the mark. Apparently, a virus was passing through the day care like wildfire, with fever and vomiting taking their toll on the victims. If the lady were right, Dee would probably have it by tomorrow. Which meant he'd be away from the office for at least two days, and that was if he didn't catch the bug, too. "Come on," he urged. "Daddy is going to get his computer and then we'll head home and rest." He attempted to sound positive.

"I don't want to rest," Dee said. "I want to play, but there's nobody to play with."

Emmie dropped her head to his shoulder, mumbled, "Daddy," and then closed her eyes.

Mitch eased her downy curls aside and kissed her warm forehead then found a little relief that it didn't seem as hot as it had when he picked her up from the day care. Maybe the children's Tylenol had already kicked in. "I'm getting you home soon, sweetie," he whispered, and then to Dee, "I'll play a game with you at home, okay?" He wasn't sure how he'd pull that off with so much work to do. Plus he'd planned to get a few groceries this afternoon before he picked them up. Now he had to take them home when there was virtually no food in the house. And he couldn't very well drag them through the grocery store.

God, please, help me.

Any other time he could call Bo and Maura, his in-laws, and they'd help with the girls. Or Hannah and Matt, his sister-in-law and her husband. But the remainder of his wife's family had headed out of town for a week at the beach following the end of the school year like many Claremont families determined to enjoy the kids' first weeks of freedom. Naturally, they'd invited Mitch to come, but he did have a lot of work...and going on vacations with Jana's family had seemed odd ever since her death.

It wasn't as if the family didn't want to include him, but Mitch found himself miserably lonely and spending his entire vacation thinking about what might have been. Or wondering what life would be like now if he were a normal twenty-nine-year-old, with two beautiful little girls and a loving wife who'd help him with the day-to-day activities of raising them. And at times like this, when they were sick.

"Daddy, I think she's going to..." Dee's warning came at the same time that the door opened and a petite dark-haired woman stepped inside his office.

"Oh, hello, I wanted to see if the position was still—" she started, but Mitch didn't hear anything else. Emmie's tummy started convulsing, her wail piercing as she attempted to get sick, dry heaves causing her little body to shake while Dee shouted, "Oh, no! Oh, no! Oh, no! Daddy, run!"

Mitch grabbed his jacket from the back of his desk chair and held it beneath his baby's mouth as he darted to the bathroom at the rear of the office.

Chapter Two

Kate watched as Mitch took the crying baby toward the back of the small building and then disappeared into what she assumed was the restroom. She could hear his soothing words echoing down the short hallway.

"It's okay, Emmie. Daddy's here."

He'd hardly acknowledged Kate before rushing the sick child away, but she hadn't detected any recognition in the brief glance. Then again, she'd only been introduced to him once three years ago. Typically, a girl would know her husband's friends well. But Kate's relationship with Chad hadn't been typical, and that was entirely her fault. Their Vegas wedding, which she'd urged him to have, had happened without the attendance of any friends. And when he'd moved her from Atlanta to Claremont in an effort to save their marriage, she'd blurted the news that nearly destroyed him and then hightailed it back to the city in a matter of days.

The only other person remaining in the front office turned wide blue eyes to Kate and shrugged small shoulders. "Emmie's sick."

Kate hadn't been around many children, so she wasn't all that certain how to respond. "I'm sorry," she said, figuring an apology wouldn't hurt.

"Yeah." Red pigtails bobbed up and down as she released an exaggerated sigh of disappointment. "Everybody's sick, and I don't have anyone to play with."

"I'm sorry," Kate repeated, and wished she had something intelligent—or at least somewhat motherly—to say.

Mitch's words were suddenly muted by the sound of running water in the bathroom. Kate could no longer understand him, but the little girl apparently did.

"Daddy's trying to get her to stop crying, but Emmie is sad. It makes you sad to be sick."

Kate couldn't agree more. "Yes, it does."

Seeing that they now agreed on something, the girl lifted one corner of her mouth and asked, "Are you Snow White? You look like Snow White." She squinted a little as though trying to reconcile Kate as the beloved character. "Yep, you look like her a lot."

Kate's smile lifted her cheeks. Jet-black hair, fair white skin—why hadn't she thought of the resemblance before?

Because in my mind, I'm still blonde and tan.

The little girl's brows lifted while she waited for an answer.

"No, I'm not," Kate said, though she didn't mind the child relating her to someone she obviously liked. "I'm…" She felt odd merely saying *Kate,* so she pulled from her own youth and added the Southern salutation. "I'm Miss Kate."

The little girl wrinkled her nose, sending a tiny spray of freckles dancing. "That's okay, I guess. But I like Snow White better."

Kate laughed. "Me, too." She was glad for the chance to chat with this little princess while waiting to talk to her dad. Her nerves had almost disappeared with the interaction, and the fact that Mitch didn't seem to remember her didn't hurt, either. "So, what's your name?" she asked.

"Dee." She moved to the smaller of the two desks in the office, put her back against the front wooden panel and then slid down to sit on the floor. She wore a yellow shirt with tiny pink flowers, matching yellow shorts and brown buckled sandals. Pink bows capped her strawberry pigtails. "Dee Ellen Gillespie," she added, her *s* coming out with an adorable lisp that made the name sound like *Gillethpie*.

As soon as Kate heard the name, she remembered even more about the time she'd met Mitch. He was with his wife, and she held their baby, a little girl only a couple of months older than Kate's daughter. Was this that little girl? Kate took a nearby seat and asked, "How old are you, Dee?"

Concentrating, she put her thumb and pinkie together and held up the middle three fingers. "This many." Then she released her pinkie finger. "But I'm almost this many. That's four."

Kate's heart tugged in her chest. Three, and almost four. This *was* the baby she remembered, almost exactly the same age as Lainey, who would be four on August 30.

Wow. Kate's daughter would be like this little girl, full of ideas and opinions and able to express herself and carry on a conversation with her mom.

But the only mom Lainey knew...wasn't Kate.

The door to the restroom opened, and Mitch came out carrying Emmie, her head on his shoulder and her eyes closed, thumb stuck in her mouth. He looked exactly like Kate remembered, with reddish hair and a ruddy complexion, bright blue eyes and broad shoulders. A strong resemblance to Prince Harry, in Kate's opinion, and the exact type of look she'd never take an interest in for herself. She'd always gone for the Bradley Cooper, Matthew McConaughey, good-looking-enough-to-stop-traffic kind of guy. But that didn't matter now anyway, because Mitch was married, and Kate wasn't here for any romantic interest. She'd chased after what she thought was love in Atlanta, and when the going got tough, Dr. Harrison Tinsdale had checked his bedside manner at the door. Then again, as a world-renowned plastic surgeon, he dealt with "pretty" on a regular basis; he had no concept of how to deal with "sick."

Mitch's eyes glanced right past Kate and zeroed in on the little girl still sitting against the desk. "Dee, you okay?"

"Yep." She bobbed her head. "She's not Snow White, though. She's just Miss Kate."

His eyes warmed toward the little girl, and then he turned his attention to Kate. "I'm afraid it isn't always this eventful in my office, but I was called to get Emmie—" he tilted his head toward the little girl now sleeping on his shoulder "—at day care because she's sick." A lift of his mouth. "I guess you figured that out."

"She going to be okay?" Kate asked.

"I'll get her home so she can rest, and then hopefully she will be. The teacher said there's a twenty-four-hour bug going around." He looked toward the bigger desk. "I'm afraid I was just stopping by to get my computer so I could work from home while I'm taking care of her. I wasn't prepared for customers, but if you want to write down your name and number, I can call you later to answer any insurance questions you may have. Are you looking for coverage? You must be new to Claremont."

"I am," Kate said. In fact, she'd crossed the city line only an hour ago. "My name is Kate Wydell. But I'm not here for insurance. I'm actually here for the position you advertised in the paper. I have a résumé." She'd nearly forgotten that she still clutched it in her hand. She lifted the résumé.

He winced. "You said that earlier, didn't you? That you were here for the job."

"Yeah, she did," Dee said, fiddling with one of the buckles on her sandals.

He gave Dee a grin, then to Kate said, "Sorry about that. My mind was on taking care of Emmie."

"That's fine." She admired the fact that he was so dedicated to his little girls. Obviously they took priority over the potential employee. Kate wished she'd have put her own little girl as a priority three years ago, but she'd attempt to rectify that now, starting with a move to Claremont and a place in Lainey's world. "Is the job still available?"

"It is," he said. "And to be honest, I've never needed help more than I do right now. I'm behind on, well, pretty much everything and—" he patted Emmie's back "—it looks like I may be taking a couple of days to work from home. Let me get my things, and I'll take your résumé with me." He turned toward the larger desk, which Kate now noticed had his nameplate perched at one corner, balanced Emmie a little more solidly in his arm and then used his opposite hand to close his laptop. Then he lifted a black computer bag from the back of the desk and started trying to put the laptop in one-handed.

Kate wasn't certain whether the feat could be accomplished while holding his baby, and she could tell he wasn't about to put the sleeping child down, so she quickly moved to stand beside him. "Here, let me help."

He already had the computer in his grasp, and her hands brushed against his as she opened the case and guided the computer inside.

She zipped the bag and then realized that she was standing closer to him than she'd intended, his height catching her off guard as she looked up into blue eyes framed with reddish-blond lashes. The contrasting color only emphasized the brightness of his eyes, as well as the compassion of a daddy holding his little girl. Kate swallowed and felt another tug of her heart. This was a real parent, what she desperately wanted to be.

Mitch cleared his throat. "Thanks."

He was thrown by the instant awareness of the woman standing so near. She was several inches shorter than Mitch, but it was her petite features, her tiny hands touching his as she helped him with the laptop, that made him feel taller. He grasped Emmie, protecting his sick baby girl by holding her close as she slept, but he found himself feeling the oddest sensation that this pretty lady needed protection, too.

And he felt another sensation as well, something he hadn't experienced in quite some time. His skin bristled with the awareness of a definite attraction to the dark-haired beauty standing so near.

A sharp stab of guilt pierced his heart and he swallowed through the assault. He'd lost Jana only a year and a half ago, merely two weeks after they'd had Emmie. He wasn't ready to feel attraction again. Didn't know if he'd ever be ready.

He was exhausted from all of the work he'd had this week and worried about his little girl. Therefore, he wasn't himself. That had to be what caused this unwanted feeling toward a woman he'd just met.

"Can we go home now?" Dee asked, pulling him out of the momentary trance.

He took a slight but noticeable step back from the woman. "Yes, we should be heading home," he said, and wrapped his fingers around the handle of his computer bag.

"You want me to put my résumé in your bag?" she asked. She'd placed the single page on the desk while she assisted him with the laptop and neither of them had thought to add it.

"Sure."

And again, soft hands brushed his as he released the handle and she quickly unzipped the bag, slid the paper in and then closed it. Mitch winced through the realization that even the touch of her hands caused an awareness he didn't need or want.

"Do you think you'll be making a decision soon? I have four years of experience as an office manager, although it was a medical office, but I do know word processing and can definitely stay calm in a crisis situation."

Mitch had been looking for someone to help out in his office for over a month. A few high schoolers had applied, saying they wanted to work in the summer but then would need to head back to school. And they'd also wanted a couple of weeks off for family vacation, mission trips or cheer camp. No one over twenty had walked through his door, and no one had any experience. This lady had four years?

"You did stay calm when I bolted to the back with Emmie," he said, thinking God may have answered his prayer…but also given him something he wasn't ready to handle. He found himself glancing to the embroidered Bible verse his mother-in-law had given him on his first Christmas without his wife, framed and hanging directly behind his desk.

God is faithful. He will not let you be tried beyond what you are able to bear.

"Yes, I did stay calm," she agreed, and then smiled.

Her smile caught him off guard because it transformed her unique face into something beautiful. Fair skin, blue eyes, jet-black curls.

Mitch wasn't so certain this was something

he could bear. Could he push the bizarre attraction aside in order to hire someone who may be exactly what he needed to help him run this office...and have more time with his girls?

Her hands still rested on the computer bag, and Mitch waited until she moved them away. No need for another awkward physical contact toward his potential employee, because he *was* thinking about hiring her...and dealing with this whatever-it-was. If God had sent this lady as an answer to Mitch's prayers, then God would also help him control this unusual response to her presence. The bottom line was that he needed help. And he wanted to be able to leave this place when Dee and Emmie needed him. "I'll call your references tonight. If everything checks out, you could start tomorrow," he said. "Would tomorrow be too soon? Like I said, I really do need some help." A major understatement.

"Tomorrow would be great."

"Dee, you ready to go? I need to get home and get some work done." And put a little space between himself and his potential employee, for now.

She clamored up from the floor. "Just work? Or can we play some, too?"

"We'll play something," he assured her, hoping that Emmie's tummy would stay settled and that he could somehow take care of her, play a game or two with Dee and also get all of today's policies updated before midnight. He really did need some help.

They left the office, and he began putting Emmie in her car seat while Dee stood nearby waiting for her turn.

"Miss Kate," Dee said, and the lady stopped walking toward her car.

"Yes?"

"You can help me get in my seat."

Mitch had started buckling Emmie, but his hands fumbled over the fastener. He looked up in time to see the lady smile at his little girl and change direction to walk toward his car.

"I'd love to help you," she said, her voice filled with so much compassion that Mitch thought she seemed on the verge of tears. He focused on her eyes, blinking more than normal and definitely fighting whatever emotion Dee's request had evoked.

Mitch was fighting one himself, because other than their family members, Dee didn't typically ask for help from anyone but her daddy. He kept his attention on securing Emmie, now snoring softly, into her seat, but looked up to lock gazes with Kate. Her dark, unruly hair framed her petite face as she focused on buckling Dee in and then gave his daughter a smile.

"How's that?" she asked.

Dee examined the buckle on her car seat and nodded. "You did good."

Kate's face practically glowed at Dee's praise. "Thanks." Then she looked up, caught Mitch staring, and they both quickly got out of the close space and shut their respective car doors.

"I'll call you after I've spoken with your references," he said, attempting to sound as professional as possible given whatever had just passed between them.

It'd been eighteen months since he'd felt anything remotely near to this. Maybe it was because she was someone new, someone who wasn't from Claremont and didn't know him as the young widower in town, as Jana's husband, or as Dee and Emmie's dad. Those were the references to him nowadays, and rarely did he simply feel like Mitch. But he didn't want to give up his new monikers because giving them up meant letting go of Jana.

Wasn't happening.

"Can you tell me something before you go?" Kate asked.

Mitch paused, his hand on the door handle. "Sure."

"I'm going to stay at the town's bed-and-breakfast until I find a place to rent. Can you give me some easy directions to—" she pulled a small slip of paper from her pocket "—111 Maple Street?"

Mitch nodded. "It's easy to find, only three miles away, but it'd be even easier for me to show you, since I live across the street from the B and B. You can follow me."

Another one of those mesmerizing smiles blindsided him again. "Thanks!"

Mitch climbed in the car, buckled up and then checked the rearview mirror to see Emmie still sleeping and Dee looking directly at him in the mirror.

"I like Miss Kate," she said.

"I do, too," he admitted. Which was good. He would need to like his employee, as long as he made sure to control the extent of that "like."

Dee peered out the window and waved to Kate before Mitch put the car in Reverse and backed up. "She's like Snow White," she said.

Mitch thought of Dee's favorite story and of the lady who seemed out of her element and took care of everyone she met. And maybe that was why God had plopped Kate Wydell in his world. He needed to simply thank Him and accept the fact that he might finally have someone to relieve the workload at the office. "Maybe," he said, "she is."

Chapter Three

Annette Tingle walked ahead of Kate toward the last room on the second floor of the bed-and-breakfast. "I know you said you wanted a small room, but this is the only one that we have available for an extended stay."

"I'll be looking for a house to rent," Kate said, "but I'm assuming I won't be able to move in until the first of the month."

"That's probably true," the lady agreed. "Hard to believe it's nearly June already. The year is flying by, isn't it?"

"Yes, it is," Kate said. Life, in fact, had flown over the past year and a half.

"Well, this is your room." Annette opened the door to a spacious bedroom complete with a canopied four-poster bed. A simple old-fashioned coverlet topped the mattress with embroidered pillows in shades of blue and rose adding a subdued hint of color. An enormous bay window with a window seat upholstered in the same shades overlooked Maple Street and consequently offered a direct view to the antebellum home across the street, the one where she'd watched Mitch pull in a short while ago.

Unable to stop herself, she walked to the big window, peered at his home and wondered how he and the girls were doing.

"Your bathroom is connected through this doorway," Mrs. Tingle said from behind her, "and you have extra linens in your closet if you need them at night. We'll charge you the regular room rate, even though this is master-sized, since that's what you'd have preferred."

"Thank you," Kate said, still focusing on the house across the street.

"And you said you're moving to Claremont?" Mrs. Tingle asked, causing Kate to reluctantly turn away from the window. She'd so enjoyed her time with Mitch's little girls. Maybe that was an indication that she *could* be a good mother, which was the entire reason she was here. "Are you here for a job, or family?" the woman continued.

Kate swallowed. *Family* would be the most correct answer, a little girl who was the same age as Dee Gillespie and whom Kate had abandoned nearly four years ago. But she wasn't ready to divulge that colossal secret. She focused on answering the woman's question instead of breaking down in tears. "I've applied for a job at Gillespie Insurance Agency as an office manager."

Mrs. Tingle clasped her hands together. "Well, that's wonderful. I'm so glad Mitch is getting some help. He's been trying to find someone for quite a while now, but it's a small town, you know. Not a lot of people with the kind of experience he needed. I told him that someone would turn up, though, and here you are." She smiled so broadly she practically beamed.

"Yes, here I am," Kate said, her voice raspy with emotion. Would Mitch still be so happy about her presence when he realized that Kate was the one who had hurt his friend?

"That young man stays so busy with work and raising his girls by himself and everything," Annette said. "It'll be good for him to have some help in that office. He's our neighbor, you know, lives just across the street."

"I know," Kate said, wondering why Mitch was raising his girls "by himself." "I was putting my résumé in at his office and asked him where I could locate the B and B, and he told me I could follow him, since he lived across from y'all."

Mrs. Tingle frowned. "He's home already? That's surprising. It's only four-thirty. He usually doesn't finish at his office until five o'clock, then he goes to get his girls and then comes home." She waved a hand in front of her face. "I bet that sounds like I'm nosy. I'm not, really. It's just that L.E. and I try to watch after our neighbors, and they do the same for us. Mitch has a fairly regular schedule. Usually he doesn't come home until his day is done."

"His little girl was sick, so he went home early," Kate said, then explained, "I'd stopped by to drop off my résumé, and he was there getting his computer so he could work at home."

The worry on Annette's face was instant. "Oh, bless that boy's heart. I wonder if he's got some soup for her. I bet he doesn't. And some food for himself. If he's trying to work from home and take care of both of the girls, too, he'll need help, especially if one is sick." She paused. "Which one is sick?"

"Emmie," Kate said, touched by the concern the woman showed toward her neighbor.

"Poor little Emmie," Annette said. "Well, okay, I'd normally have L.E. take some things over for them, but he's gone to Stockville to pick up some supplies. And I've got a few more guests that are supposed to arrive within the next hour, so I shouldn't leave. Do you think you'd mind running a little care package over to Mitch from us, dear? You did meet him already, right?"

"I did, and I'd be happy to." In fact, she hadn't been able to get the girls off her mind. Emmie was so sick, and Dee had seemed sad that her daddy's attention would have to be focused on his youngest daughter instead of playing with her. Following along as the woman returned to the hallway, Kate thought of Mitch, holding Emmie and promising Dee that he'd find a way to play a game with her, too. What a wonderful parent he was, someone whom she could watch and learn from, for sure. Because she desperately wanted to be a parent, a wonderful parent, to Lainey. If Chad would give her a chance.

Annette stopped halfway down the hall and indicated a different staircase than the one they'd taken earlier. "This leads to the kitchen," she said, heading down with Kate following in her wake. "So if you ever get hungry for a snack or would like iced tea or coffee, it'll always be available for you down here. But for now, we'll use it to get some things together for Mitch and the girls." She crossed the room and removed a patchwork quilt from the top of a chest freezer.

Kate moved to stand beside her and got there just in time for Annette to fill her arms.

"Here we go," she said, handing her a large bowl labeled *Chicken Noodle Soup.* Then she balanced a Ziploc bag labeled *Corn Bread* on top of the bowl. And then she withdrew another flat container with *Pecan Pie* written across the side. "You can take the soup over to the microwave for me, if you don't mind," she said. "There's a defrost button we can use for that and the corn bread. We'll have everything ready to eat, in case they're all hungry now." She continued rummaging through all of the labeled containers in the freezer.

Kate nodded. "Okay." She found the oversize microwave, took the lid off the soup container and then started defrosting. She found it oddly comforting to hear the woman instruct her around the kitchen. She hadn't had those experiences growing up that she often saw in commercials or on paintings, where the little apron-clad girl stood on a chair beside her mom and poured the chocolate chips into the cookie batter. Her stepmom hadn't liked the kids in the kitchen, so Kate's first attempts at cooking hadn't occurred until she was in her first apart-

ment. Assisting Annette Tingle in the kitchen
touched her heart, and again, she found herself
swallowing past tears. Wouldn't it be something
if she could help her own little girl make cook-
ies one day?

By the time Annette joined her with a breakfast casserole and another large bowl labeled
Potato Soup, Kate had harnessed her emotions,
defrosted the soup and corn bread and was moving on to the pie.

"We'll just defrost the pie and leave it that
way for him to put in and heat up a piece at
a time. But the soup and corn bread we'll go
ahead and heat so it's ready to go," Annette
said, taking the other frozen items in her hand
with her to a set of side shelves organized with
plates, cups, utensils and a couple of picnic
baskets. She brought the largest basket to the
table, placed the potato soup and casserole in
the bottom and then situated several red-and-
white-checked fabric napkins over them. "We'll
put the heated things on top, and you can let
him know to put the food for tomorrow in his
fridge." She smiled. "That'll help him out a bit.
He's such a sweet man and a great daddy to his
girls. I'm sure you will enjoy working for him,
too."

Kate continued heating the food for tonight

but found the courage to ask what she wanted to know most. "You said he takes care of the girls all by himself?" She attempted to sound nonchalant. She remembered meeting the pretty lady who had been Mitch's wife three years ago, though she couldn't recall her name. And she also remembered that the two had appeared very much in love and absolutely thrilled with their little baby. Dee.

"Oh, yes," Annette said, placing the pie in the basket and putting more napkins around it while making room for the soup and corn bread. "I'm sorry. I wasn't thinking that you wouldn't know. I'm sure Mitch wouldn't mind me telling you since you'll find out soon enough working for him and all. He's a widower, poor dear. His sweet wife, Jana, had breast cancer, and it got really bad when she was carrying little Emmie. She wouldn't have treatments while she was pregnant because she was afraid, you know, chemo and radiation might hurt the baby."

"But you can be treated while you're pregnant," Kate said. She didn't explain why she knew. Luckily, the lady didn't ask.

"Oh, I know. That's what they told Jana and Mitch, but she was so afraid that it might hurt the baby that she didn't want to risk it. You know, they're always finding out new things, and she didn't want to be treated and then find out later that they just didn't realize it'd hurt Emmie."

"And the cancer got worse?" Kate guessed.

Annette pulled the steaming soup from the microwave and put it on top of the napkins in the basket. "By the time Emmie came, there wasn't any chance of survival. Jana lived a couple of weeks after the baby was born."

Kate's stomach pitched. A year ago, she'd thought that she wouldn't have the chance to ever see her little girl. Mitch's wife had barely met Emmie before she died. "That had to be so hard for him."

"It was hard on him and on the whole town really," she said. "Everyone loved Jana. Her family has lived in this town for as long as I can remember. And everyone loves Mitch." She placed the corn bread in the basket and closed the lid, then winked at Kate. "We all try to take care of him and those girls. That's the way this town is, you know. Everyone is like family."

Kate nodded, remembering Chad trying to sell her on the move to Claremont by saying that very thing. And remembering how she'd stayed here only a few days before leaving him, the town he loved and her baby girl behind.

"So would you mind taking this over to him?"

Annette asked. "And I'll finish getting those other rooms ready for our guests."

"I'm happy to do it," Kate said, meaning every word.

Mitch poured apple juice into Dee's sippy cup and handed it to her while he looked at the bare shelves of his refrigerator. He had eggs, so he could scramble some for dinner. That should be easy enough on Emmie's stomach. But then if he cooked those tonight, what would they have for breakfast in the morning?

"Daddy, I'm hungry," Dee said, echoing his problem.

"How about an apple to hold you over until I can get something fixed for dinner?" He plucked one out of the fruit bowl.

She frowned. "I want green this time," she said, then added, "please."

Mitch returned the Red Delicious and retrieved a Granny Smith apple from the bowl. Lately he'd noticed her voicing her opinions and making more decisions on her own, displaying the independence and confidence that he'd always admired in her mom. He couldn't be more proud. "One green apple coming up."

"Thanks, Daddy."

"You're welcome."

She watched as he sliced the apple, put it on her Dora the Explorer plate and placed it in front of her at the kitchen table. Emmie had been asleep ever since they got home, but he expected her to wake soon. She'd be hungry and thirsty, and he wanted to make sure he was prepared.

"Maybe I'll go ahead and have some eggs ready for when Emmie wakes up," he said to Dee.

Dee, chomping happily on her apple, nodded. "Yep, that'll be good. You want to play a game while she's still asleep?"

"Sure." He'd kind of hoped she would forget the game promise for a while, at least until he got a few of those policies checked out, but he didn't want to let her down, and playing while Emmie was asleep was probably the best route to take, since Emmie would undoubtedly not want to leave his arms once she woke. Which would also make it impossible for him to get his work done.

Help me out, here, Lord. You know I need it.

Mitch almost didn't hear the tiny tap from the front of the house, but Dee did.

"Someone's here," she said, abandoning the apple and crawling off her seat to run toward the front of the house. She was probably hoping it was one of her friends coming to play. Mandy and Daniel Brantley occasionally brought Kaden over, and Chad and Jessica Martin visited every now and then with Lainey. But the majority of Dee's friends were out of town with their families. Mitch had considered letting the girls go along with their grandparents on the family trip, but he simply hadn't wanted to part with them for that long. Now, with Emmie's sickness, he was glad he'd kept them home. But somehow, he'd need to find a way to combat Dee's boredom with their current situation. Maybe whoever was at the door would help.

By the time he got to the foyer, Dee had already started reaching for the doorknob. Naturally, it was locked, but even so, he wanted her to remember the rule. "Wait, sweetie. Daddy needs to open the door, remember?"

"Okay." She'd already moved to the sidelight, pulled the skinny curtain aside and peered out. "Hey! It's Miss Kate!"

At the sound of Kate's name, Mitch realized that he'd actually hoped to see her again tonight. He'd planned to call her and let her know he'd talked to her references, but telling her in person would be better. He didn't know why he felt that way, but he wasn't about to try to analyze it.

He unlocked and opened the wooden door,

which left the screen door separating Mitch and Dee from their visitor.

"What you got in the basket, Miss Kate?" Dee bounced in place while she waited for Mitch to open the screen door.

Kate clutched the handles of an oversize picnic basket with both hands. From the strained look on her face, the thing was pretty heavy.

Mitch pushed the door open and hurried to take the large basket.

Kate smiled. "Thanks. I don't think I could've stood here holding it much longer."

"What have you got in here?" he asked, turning to go back into the house.

"It's from Mrs. Tingle," she called, and Mitch realized she still stood on the porch.

"Come on in!" Dee said, waving her inside, and Mitch nodded his agreement.

"Yes, forgive me. Please come in." He led the way to the kitchen, where he placed the basket on the table then opened the lid to release the most amazing aromas he'd smelled in this kitchen in months.

"Oh, that smells good," Dee said, climbing up on her seat to peer into the basket.

"It's chicken noodle soup, corn bread and pecan pie for your dinner," Kate said, as Mitch removed each of the named items from the basket.

He lifted an abundance of checked napkins and then saw more containers on the bottom.

"That's a breakfast casserole and potato soup for tomorrow," Kate said. "Mrs. Tingle said she didn't want you to worry about cooking."

"That lady spoils me," Mitch said, grinning, "but I'm not about to complain."

"She seems very sweet," Kate agreed.

He placed the hot items on the stove and the cold ones in the fridge. Then he turned to see Kate standing awkwardly near the table as though she weren't certain whether to stay or to leave. Mitch didn't know whether he should politely usher her out or follow an instinct he didn't quite understand…and ask her to stay.

It turned out, the decision wasn't really his to make. Dee took over.

"Daddy has to work but I really want to play a game. Would you play a game with me?"

Kate's eyes lifted and found Mitch's. "Would that be okay with you?"

"If you wouldn't mind, that'd be fine. I'm sure Dee would like it." He'd like it, too, actually. He did have a lot of work to do, but he hadn't wanted to let his little girl down.

"Yes, I sure would," Dee said. "I can get my Memory game. Do you like the Memory game?"

"I'm not sure, but we'll see," Kate said.

"Okay!" Dee jumped off her chair and darted out of the kitchen toward the game room.

Mitch found himself alone with Kate. She eased into a chair at the table and nervously pulled at one of her black curls.

"Are you sure you don't mind staying here a little while to play Memory with her?" he asked. "I can promise you she won't be satisfied with one game, and I should also tell you she's pretty good and doesn't tend to show mercy."

A small laugh escaped. "I was just hoping you didn't feel like I was trying to bombard your space or take away from your time with your girls." One corner of her mouth lifted along with a shoulder. "Or try to sway you into feeling like you have to hire me because I've won Dee over."

"I'll admit it doesn't hurt that she likes you so much already," he said. "But truthfully, I called your references as soon as I got home, and they all sang your praises. Just be forewarned that Dee and Emmie come with the territory. Playing games and having tea parties may actually end up being a part of your job description."

Her eyes practically danced. "Oh, Mr. Gillespie, I can't tell you how much I'd enjoy that."

"Mitch," he corrected. "Please call me Mitch."

She blinked, and he saw something pass over

her face that he didn't understand, as though maybe she were debating them being on a first-name basis. But it didn't mean anything. Everyone in Claremont went by first names. And thankfully, she nodded. "Okay. Mitch. I can't tell you how much I'd enjoy that as a part of my job description."

Dee bounded into the room with the game clutched in her hands, and he watched the two flip the square pieces over on the table. Dee's excited chatter and Kate's gentle words to his daughter filled the kitchen, but Mitch heard only one thing.

Kate Wydell…saying his name.

Chapter Four

Mitch quietly stepped away from Dee's room so he wouldn't wake her from her nap. His oldest princess had tried to deny the virus had gotten the best of her, saying that she was not going to let Emmie's "bad bug" make her sick, too.

But as Mitch suspected, yesterday afternoon, when Emmie had begun to feel better, Dee's stomach had started, in her words, "feeling yucky." And then, like Emmie, she hadn't been able to keep any food down. Today, after two full days of taking care of the girls, it seemed the worst of the virus was thankfully behind them.

And he was thankful for his new employee's willingness to spend her first couple of days on the job working from Mitch's front porch. The weather, in the low seventies with a frequent breeze, had made their temporary work environment quite enjoyable, and Mitch was glad for the ability to keep the office running remotely while also personally taking care of his girls.

He'd kept the wooden front door open throughout the day so he could listen for Dee through the screen one. Now he took advantage of that from the opposite side as he listened to Kate speak to one of his clients, her fingers tapping the keys of her laptop while she cradled the phone between her right ear and shoulder.

"Yes, Mrs. Tolleson," she said, "I'll be happy to let you know how much that would cost. I just need a little more information about your son."

Mitch stopped walking and watched her capably select the website path to obtain a quote for renter's insurance. And while Kate followed through the standard questions about the son's age, address, marital status and home-contents value, Mitch studied the picturesque scene of his front porch.

A few feet from Kate, Emmie dozed peacefully in her pack-and-play, the mesh sides allowing Mitch to see one tiny hand clutching her nighty-night, the blanket Jana had sewn for her while she was pregnant. She'd created the satin border from one of her blouses and had said she hoped it'd somehow keep her close to her baby after she was gone.

Whether Emmie realized the fabric was from her mommy or not, the blanket was a must-have whenever she slept. Her opposite hand was balled near her chin with her tiny lips subtly moving around her thumb. The image would make a beautiful painting, but Mitch would be lying if he said that the sleeping child was the only thing worthy of a painting on his front porch. He turned his attention to the woman still speaking softly on the phone, her quiet tone obviously due to the sleeping baby.

A couple of decorative, very feminine bobby pins held back Kate's dark curls on each side. Like yesterday, her outfit was dressy enough to qualify as business-casual but also appeared comfortable and modest. Today she wore a short white crocheted jacket over a sleeveless sky-blue dress that reached her ankles. Small pearls dotted each ear and a matching single-pearl necklace rested against her throat. She wore minimal makeup, only a hint of eye shadow and a pale pink lipstick, from what Mitch could tell. He wasn't an expert on makeup or anything, but it seemed that the small amount only accented her blue eyes and heart-shaped lips.

Definitely an image worthy of a painting.

He swallowed. She was pretty. Very pretty. Unnervingly pretty. But he wasn't certain whether it was the fact that he noticed her attractiveness that bothered him or the fact that he found himself appreciating scenes like this, where she sat comfortably on the top porch step, her dress sweeping the stairs and her back leaning against the wood column as she worked and occasionally smiled at his sleeping baby.

She looked like a sweet young mother.

A sharp stab of guilt slammed him. Jana should be here, on this porch, smiling at her daughter and being the center of Mitch's world. Then this scene might actually be real, a part of his life, instead of an instance where an employee worked at his home to help him through a difficult situation.

Maybe he should have pushed harder to have Jana take the chemo treatments during the pregnancy. Maybe then she'd be here now, and he wouldn't be thinking about how things would be if he had a woman in his life.

He shook his head. He'd been doing fine raising the girls on his own, and just because this scene with Kate seemed picture-perfect, that didn't mean he needed someone else, not to be a mother to his girls or to be a—

He didn't finish the thought. Several friends had asked about his plans for the future over the past couple of months, specifically whether

he saw himself dating again, marrying again.
Each time, he'd said no. And he'd meant it. He
still loved Jana, would always love Jana. This
awkward feeling around Kate didn't mean anything. He simply hadn't been around a female
for an extended period of time since Jana passed
away. Plus all of the ladies from Claremont
still thought of him as "Jana's Mitch." Mitch
liked that. Really. And thankfully, Kate hadn't
seemed to show any interest in him beyond a
working relationship. He liked that, too.

Really.

Emmie made a smacking noise as she pulled
her thumb from her mouth, stretched and rolled
over. Mitch stepped toward the screen door so
he could pick her up when she woke, but before
he got there, Kate finished her call and smiled
at the little girl reaching both arms toward the
woman on the porch.

"Kay-Kay," Emmie said, her eyes still heavy
with sleep and her soft strawberry curls standing on end.

Kate closed her laptop and placed it to the
side then eased toward the edge of the playpen.
"Hey, there, sweetie. Did you have a good rest?"

Mitch held his breath as she picked up
Emmie, and his little girl contentedly rested
her head against Kate's slender shoulder.

She gently patted Emmie's back. "I'll hold you now," she said, "and Daddy will be back in a second. He went to check on your sister."

"Kay-Kay," Emmie repeated as she snuggled in Kate's arms. Mitch couldn't help but notice it was the same tone she used when he picked her up from her nap and she said, "Daddy."

He cleared his throat and prepared to take over, but then he heard tiny feet approaching from behind him.

"I woked up," Dee said.

Mitch turned as she reached him, her blue eyes blinking as they adjusted to the sunlight filtering into the hallway from the screen door. Picking her up, he kissed her cheek, no longer warm from fever. "Yes, you did," he said. "Did you sleep well?"

She nodded. "I feel better," she said, then with a yawn asked, "Can we play?"

His laugh surprised him. He'd felt ill at ease watching Kate interact with Emmie, but Dee's arrival had squelched his unease and brought him back to what was important, the fact that both of his little girls were starting to feel better. And the fact that he had a capable new employee who'd been willing to help him out when he was in a bind.

Lord, help me continue to see the good in all

*of this instead of feeling guilty over something
that I can't change.*

"Daddy." Emmie spied Mitch and Dee as they
neared the screen door. She didn't make any
effort to reach for him, probably because he
was already holding Dee, or maybe because she
seemed quite content in Kate's arms.

"Hey, sweetie," Mitch answered. He pushed
the door open and stepped onto the porch. The
breeze carried the faint scent of peaches, which
Mitch had determined over the past two days
as the fragrance of Kate's perfume. The smell
suited the woman holding Emmie. Sweet and
tender. A good-hearted woman and a diligent
employee. He needed to stop seeing the way
she fit in with his girls as a bad thing and realize that God had given him exactly what he'd
asked for.

Thank You, Lord.

"I feel better now," Dee pronounced.

Mitch smiled. He felt better now, too.

"I think I can play now," she continued. She
seemed to direct the statement toward Kate,
which made sense, since Kate had played several games with her before she'd gotten sick.

Kate grinned. "Nothing overly exertive, I'd
think, but maybe something low-key."

"What's 'over zertive'?" she asked.

Mitch grinned. "That's a little much for a three-year-old's vocabulary," he said quietly to Kate. Then to Dee, he said, "Miss Kate just means that you should take it easy, since your tummy hasn't felt too good the past couple of days. Maybe not play anything that causes you to run around, like hide-and-seek. That's what 'overly exertive' means."

"Oh," Dee said with a shrug. "Okay." Then she peered down the street toward the square. "I'm hungry, too. Can we go get ice cream?"

At the mention of her favorite treat, Emmie's head lifted from Kate's shoulder. "Ice cweam?"

"Please, Daddy?" Dee asked.

He was a sucker for the way she said *please* and he was pretty sure she knew it. Even so, he grinned. They'd had a rough couple of days and deserved a treat. "You know, we are pretty much finished with the accounts for today, aren't we, Kate?" he asked.

"I actually finished the last one thirty minutes ago," she said. "But then Mrs. Tolleson called, and I wanted to get her the policy information she asked for. She seemed like a really sweet lady on the phone."

"She is. She and her husband own the variety store on the square. Maybe we will see them when we go for ice cream. So, are you at a good stopping point?" Mitch asked.

"You could go get ice cream with us?" Dee asked. "Please?"

"You want me to go, too?" Her surprise at his question was evident. For the past two days, she'd worked with him here, but she'd always walked across the street and had her meals at the B and B with the Tingles and the other guests. Asking her to eat with them at their home had seemed too personal, and Mitch had wanted to keep their relationship as professional as possible.

But this was different. His girls were feeling better, and he wanted to celebrate. It only made sense to invite the woman who'd helped them through their sickness.

"Of course I want you to go," he said. "Unless, say, you don't like ice cream?"

"You don't like ice cream?" Dee's eyes widened in shock. "Why?"

Kate laughed, causing Emmie to lift her head and smile, and then she put her hand to Kate's cheek. "Kay-Kay."

A ripple of something passed over Mitch, but he swallowed past the feeling.

"I do like ice cream," she said to Dee. "I like it very much, in fact, and I'd love to get some with all of you." She glanced at Mitch again. "If you're sure it's okay for me to go."

"Of course." He forced a laugh and hoped she saw it as a casual invitation, which was exactly what it was, nothing like a date or anything.

"Yay, Miss Kate is going, too!" Dee's high-pitched cheer delivered near Mitch's right ear caused him to flinch.

"I guess I am," Kate said, squeezing Emmie in a hug. "Let's go get some ice cream, Emmie." From the smile claiming Kate's face, he thought she might actually be more excited about the treat than his girls.

Kate waved to Mr. Tingle, trimming the azalea bushes on the side of the bed-and-breakfast, as they began the short walk to the square. She'd already grown very fond of the sweet couple that ran the B and B. They reminded her of the kind of parents anyone would want, the kind she'd never had, and the kind she wanted her own daughter to have.

She blinked past the emotion causing her throat to tense. Her little girl undoubtedly had parents like that. Would Chad and his wife be okay with her having one more? And would they believe that she could be a good mom to Lainey after what she'd done in the past?

"Look at the flowers on those trees, Miss Kate." Dee pointed to the row of Yoshino cherry trees lining Maple Street and leading to the square. The vivid pink blossoms resembled oversize roses and covered nearly every branch of the stunning trees. Her comment pulled Kate from the fear of Chad's reaction to her arrival in Claremont and brought her back to the joy of spending time with these two little girls. *This* must be what motherhood felt like. And it was wonderful.

Kate swallowed. "I do see them, and they're so pretty."

"Pretty," Emmie echoed. But she wasn't looking at the trees; instead, she patted Kate's cheek the way she'd done several times throughout the day and repeated, "Pretty."

Kate kissed her chubby cheek. "You're pretty."

"And me, too?" Dee asked. Mitch had put her down midway to the square. She still held his hand but looked at Kate for an answer.

Kate recalled the many times growing up when she asked her stepmom that very question. "Am I pretty?" And the traditional answer, a quick "You'll do."

She moved closer to Mitch and Dee so she could reach out and run a hand along the soft curl of one of Dee's pigtails as she answered, "You're very pretty, Dee. In fact, you're beautiful."

Dee's smile beamed, her walk turned into a skip and Kate felt a rush of warmth to her heart. She would *never* let her child wonder whether she were pretty. She just hoped she got the chance to tell Lainey, and soon.

"Bew-ful," Emmie said.

"Yes, you're beautiful, too." Laughing, Kate looked from Emmie to Mitch. Though he continued walking toward the town square, his eyes were focused on Kate, not merely looking at her but studying her in a way that sent a shiver down her spine. What was he thinking now? Should she not tell his girls they were beautiful? Because they were, and she so wanted to make sure they knew. "Everything okay?" she asked him.

He inhaled thickly, let it out and then nodded. "Yes, everything's fine." Then, as though he needed to say it before he changed his mind, he added, "Thank you, Kate."

Confused, she asked, "For what?"

"For helping me this week," he said, "and for reminding the girls...of what they are." He tweaked Dee's cheek. "You are beautiful."

"You're beautiful, too, Daddy!" Dee continued to skip, and her daddy grinned.

And Kate noticed that, while she might not call him *beautiful,* Mitch did have an appealing quality, especially when he looked at his girls, and occasionally…when he looked at Kate.

Mitch wiped the smear of strawberry ice cream from Emmie's chin with a napkin, and she gave him a full baby-teeth grin.

"Tank oo, Daddy."

"You're welcome," he said.

Dee had wanted to sit by Kate at the Sweet Stop candy shop while they ate their ice cream, and now that the ice cream was gone, she remained at Kate's side. "Can we take Miss Kate to see the toy store?" she asked.

Mitch gathered the abundance of used napkins from their table and, with Emmie perched on his hip, took them to the trash. "That's mighty nice of you to want to show Miss Kate the toy store," he said, knowing that the Tiny Tots Treasure Box was Dee's favorite store on the square, with the Sweet Stop running a close second. "Are you sure Miss Kate wants to see the toy store?"

"Everyone loves toys, and Miss Kate loves games, and they've got lots of games there, too." Her pigtails bobbed to emphasize the fact. "Don't you want to see it, Miss Kate?"

Kate smiled as Dee reached for her hand. "If your dad says we have time to go," she answered.

"Way to throw it back on me," he teased, but truly he didn't mind taking his girls to their beloved toy store.

Kate grinned. "Sorry, but you're the daddy, so you're the boss, right?"

Dee nodded. "Yep, he's the daddy."

Mitch held the door and tilted his head toward the square. "I guess we're going to the toy store, then."

Obviously excited to hear their new point of destination, Emmie gave him one of her open-mouthed kisses on the cheek, which Mitch was fairly certain would leave him sticky. He didn't care. He lived for those hugs.

Dee, looking as happy as Emmie, took Kate's hand and tugged her toward the sidewalk. "Come on, Miss Kate. You'll like the toy store."

"I'm sure I will," she said, passing close to Mitch as they walked through the doorway, the hint of peaches following in her wake.

"Mr. Gillespie?"

Ignoring the impulse to inhale deeper, he

turned toward the teenager who'd been working the ice cream counter. "Yes, Jasmine?"

She waited a beat as Kate moved farther away, then said, "I like her. Kate. She seems very nice."

He'd introduced Kate to the girl when they arrived and had also told her that Kate was his new employee, just in case she got the wrong idea about the four of them coming for ice cream. Had she gotten the wrong idea anyway? He glanced outside, where Dee had already tugged Kate toward the next store. "I like her, too," he said. "I think she's going to be a good employee," he added for good measure.

Jasmine's mouth dipped in a frown and her brows followed suit, giving him one of those looks girls perfected that said he didn't know what he was saying. But he did. And he wouldn't justify her curiosity by trying to explain more. As a teen, Jasmine undoubtedly romanticized everything. Eventually she'd see that he and Kate had a professional relationship and that was it. No need for the people around town to think anything more of it than that.

"Have a good day, Jasmine," he said, closing the door behind him and ignoring the fact that her frown had slid into a smile, as though she knew something he didn't.

Teenagers. In ten years, he'd have one, and then soon after, he'd have another. And by then, hopefully, he'd understand them a little better.

But he wouldn't rush his little girls getting older. He wanted to enjoy every day, every age, like they were doing today, spending time together on the square.

"Well, hello, girls," James Bowers said as they approached Bowers' Sporting Goods store. He put several fishing rods in a large red barrel on the sidewalk. "Who's your friend?"

"This is Miss Kate," Dee said. "She likes ice cream."

Kate laughed. "Yes, I do."

Mitch quickly caught up and explained, "Kate just moved here and is my new employee."

Mr. Bowers situated the rods in the barrel and then turned it so the sale sign faced the street. "Well, that's great," he said. "You've needed some help for quite a while now, haven't you?"

"Yes, I have."

"So, you came to Claremont for the job?" the man continued.

Kate blinked a couple of times, and her cheeks seemed to tinge a little more pink before she answered. "I wanted to live in a small town for a change, and Claremont seemed like a great place to settle down." She glanced around at the square. "It's lovely here."

"Been here all my life," he said, "and I haven't found any reason to complain. Met my sweetheart here when we were still kids at Claremont Elementary."

The door to the sporting goods shop opened, and Jolaine Bowers stepped out. "Well, hey, Mitch. How're you doing?" she asked.

"I'm good," Mitch answered, not missing the fact that while she spoke to Mitch, her eyes were definitely more focused on Kate.

"Your ears burning?" Her husband winked at her. "Or did you come out because you saw a new face and wanted the scoop?" He tilted his head toward Kate.

She playfully punched him in the biceps. "I'm just being friendly, James," she chided. "But I don't believe we met," she continued to Kate. "I'm Jolaine Bowers."

"Kate Wydell. I'm working for Mitch at his insurance agency now," she said, then gave a soft smile. "Well, I will be working there. I haven't actually worked at the office yet."

"We've been working from my house, since the girls have been sick this week," he said.

"Miss Kate likes ice cream," Dee said. "And playing games. And toys."

Jolaine's deep dimples pierced her cheeks as she grinned at Mitch's three-year-old. "I think that's great, Dee," she said. Then she turned her focus to Mitch and said, "I think it's wonderful, actually."

Mitch didn't have to wonder whether she had the wrong idea. She did. And the knowing look she gave him said she was probably already seeing a wedding in his near future. Maybe it wasn't just the teenagers in this town who tended to romanticize too much. And he really needed everyone to realize that Kate was his employee, nothing more. "We've had a tough couple of days," he said, "with the girls dealing with the virus going through the day care and all, and so we decided to go for ice cream. Didn't seem right not to invite Kate, since she's helped us out so much."

The couple nodded...and continued grinning.

Mitch gave up. "Well, we'll see you around," he said, and started walking away, but Jolaine halted them with her question to Kate.

"Kate, I'm assuming you don't have a church home in town yet? If not, then you should come to our midweek service tonight at Claremont Community Church. We have a great group of folks there and a wonderful preacher with Brother Henry. He teaches the auditorium class on Wednesdays." She waited a second for Kate to speak, and when she didn't, Jolaine continued, "Mitch, you and the girls will be there tonight, won't you?"

She knew he would, but Mitch went ahead and answered, "Yes."

"So he could show you where the church is," Jolaine continued, her smile managing to grow even more and those dimples sinking to oblivion with her excited grin. "We'd sure love to have you."

Kate hesitated, looking to Mitch as though trying to determine his thoughts on the invitation to church. Mitch, however, was mentally kicking himself. He hadn't thought to ask her to church. He also realized that he hadn't thought to ask her why she'd come to Claremont initially. Obviously it wasn't for the job, since she'd already arrived in town before she answered his classified ad. What would bring someone like Kate to Claremont? She'd come from Atlanta, as big a city as you could find in the South, and moved here to Tinyville, Alabama. A moment ago she'd said that she came to experience life in a small town.

Was that it? Or was there more?

"You'll like church," Dee said to Kate. "But we'll go to the toy store first."

James and Jolaine chuckled, and Mitch realized he'd yet to state his own invitation.

"Yes, you will," he said. "You can follow us to the building, if you want. We meet at seven o'clock."

"That sounds nice," Kate answered. "I had recently started attending a church that I liked in Atlanta, but I haven't had a chance to find a place to attend here. Mr. and Mrs. Tingle had mentioned their church, though, and I thought I might visit."

Mr. Bowers grinned. "Same church, so we'll see you there either way."

"That's great," Kate said, but Mitch noticed she still looked a little hesitant and not all that excited. Was faith something new in her life? And had that been a part of what brought her to Claremont?

"Toys, Daddy," Emmie said, patting his cheek with her small hand. "'Kay?"

"Okay, sweetie," he said, then told Mr. and Mrs. Bowers that they would see them tonight at church and continued across the square. But he couldn't get his thoughts off the niggling question…what really brought Kate Wydell to Claremont?

By the time they reached the toy store, Mitch had introduced his new employee to the majority of Claremont's merchants on the square, and each time they received the same look and response that they'd gotten from Mr. and Mrs. Bowers. A questioning gaze of whether there was something more to this ice cream outing quickly followed by a knowing smile that they suspected Mitch had an interest in the new girl. And then the response that bothered him most—a tender smile toward his girls that he knew meant "Oh, how wonderful it'd be if they had a mommy in their world."

That look pierced his heart. They did have a mommy. She'd been gone only a year and a half. And his girls were doing fine. So was Mitch, for that matter. He simply needed the town to realize that he could have a female employee without it being anything more, that he could take that employee for ice cream without it meaning anything more.

The string of bells on the door at the Tiny Tots Treasure Box sounded loudly as they entered.

"Welcome to Tiny Tots," Mr. Feazell, the store owner, called from where he was settling a dollhouse in the middle of a display. He placed a tiny light so that it spotlighted the house and then quickly moved to the front of the store to welcome his guests. Unfortunately, Mitch saw the older man's entire appearance change when he noticed Kate holding Dee's hand. "Well, hello," he said, grinning. "Who do you have with you today, Dee?"

"This is Miss Kate," Dee said. "She likes toys."

"You don't say. Well, it's a pleasure to meet you, Miss Kate." His head nodded subtly. "We're glad you're here. Where are you from? And how did you two meet?"

Leave it to one of the oldest men in town to toss out his filter completely and ask what everyone else was thinking. Mitch prepared to explain Kate's employee role again, but Kate spoke before he had a chance.

"Oh, no," she said, an embarrassed laugh bubbling out with her words. "It isn't like that. Mr. Gillespie is my employer. I'm working in his office, and he was kind enough to invite me to the square this afternoon with him and his girls."

Mr. Feazell had a good deal of snow-white beard covering his face, but even so, Mitch saw the tops of his cheeks redden with embarrassment at his presumption. He shook his head. "Oh, I, uh—" he chuckled "—well, I'm glad you got some help for your office, Mitch, and a right pretty helper, too, I might add." Yet another testament to the fact that Ted Feazell had no problem saying exactly what was on his mind.

Looking uncertain about how to answer, Kate simply mumbled, "Thank you," and then allowed Dee to pull her toward the dollhouse display.

"Come look, Miss Kate," she said, and Kate obliged.

"Sorry about that, Mitch. Thought you had a lady friend," Mr. Feazell said after they'd walked away. He attempted to whisper, but his ability to whisper had apparently flown out the window at the same time he lost his filter for words, and Mitch saw Kate's cheeks blush bright pink.

"No problem," Mitch said.

"Doggy." Emmie pointed to an abundance of stuffed animals lining the entire right side of the store.

Mitch walked toward the packed bins and tried to spot the one that had caught her eye. He spied a fluffy white puppy with a purple bow and pulled it from the stack.

"No," Emmie said, shaking her head and pointing again. "Doggy."

There had to be thirty dogs in the overstuffed bin she indicated, and since he wasn't entirely certain he'd gotten all of the strawberry ice cream off of her hands, he didn't want to have her running her palm across the toys, but he also didn't know how he would find the one she wanted. He lifted a brown Chihuahua.

Strawberry brows furrowed and her lower lip poked out. "No, Daddy. Dat doggy." He leaned her closer, not close enough for her to touch, but close enough that he could narrow down his selection. It appeared as though she were reaching for either a tiny black poodle or a bulldog that had one of those "so ugly it was cute" looks. He plucked the poodle out as Kate and Dee walked over, with Dee moving to the fairy-tale figures near the Disney display.

"Trouble picking one out?" Kate asked.

"Trouble with me finding the one she wants," Mitch clarified, while Mr. Feazell, standing nearby and watching it all, laughed.

Mitch couldn't imagine her wanting the other dog, with its flat face and wrinkles, but he took it from the batch, and then was shocked when Emmie began clapping.

"Yes!" She grabbed the smushed-faced toy as soon as it was within reach and promptly buried her head against its fur. "Doggy!"

"That's the one you want?" Mitch asked, but Emmie simply continued to snuggle and love the new toy. He looked at Mr. Feazell. "I guess that's the one we'll take."

But Ted Feazell's hand was over his mouth, his eyes were wide and his head shook slightly as he watched Emmie's reaction to the toy. "I'm not believing…"

Confused, Mitch looked from him to his baby girl and then back. "Not believing what?"

"It's just that, well, most little girls go for the cute puppies, you know, the fluffy ones, softer fur, that type of thing. I don't get that many bulldogs in, because girls typically don't like them, and the boys usually pick something bigger. I've only had one other little girl who ever had a fit over bulldogs like that. I remember each time she came in the store when she was little, that was what she wanted. She always said she wanted a real one someday, but she never got one."

Mitch's memory kicked into place, and he remembered his wife talking about the puppy they'd get when Dee was big enough. "Jana?" he asked.

Mr. Feazell's eyes watered, and he rubbed a weathered hand across them before nodding. "Isn't that something? She was just a baby when Jana passed, wasn't she?"

"Two weeks old," Mitch said, and he noticed

that Kate had taken a step toward them, her mouth open in surprise.

"They always say kids take after their parents in what they like and all," Mr. Feazell said. "Wouldn't have thought about that applying to toy animals, but it sure does seem to be the case, doesn't it?"

"Yes," Mitch said thickly, "it does."

"Doggy," Emmie repeated, grinning against the animal's face.

Mitch held her a little tighter and silently appreciated the fact that she'd obviously taken after Jana in what she liked. How many other things would he see and learn over the years that showed a glimpse of the woman he loved through their children?

"She likes…what her mommy liked," Kate said, almost so softly that Mitch didn't hear, but he looked up and noticed her hand held just beneath her throat as she stared awestruck at Emmie.

Mitch didn't get a chance to think too much about Kate's tender emotion at seeing Emmie's reaction to the animal because at that moment, Dee cheered, "I found her. I finally found her!" Then she ran toward them from the Disney section holding up her prized find. A tiny figurine…of Snow White.

Chapter Five

After the town's reaction to the two of them at the square this afternoon, Mitch hadn't offered for Kate to ride with them to church. No need to add fuel to the gossip fire. So instead, he'd merely let her follow them to the building, and then when they entered the lobby, he curtly introduced her to Brother Henry. While the preacher welcomed her, Mitch explained that he needed to take the girls to their respective classes.

He ignored Dee's tug on his arm as she tried to get him to wait for Miss Kate, and he ignored her complaint that she'd really wanted to show Kate her classroom. He'd also taken his time dropping the girls off at class so that his new employee would already be seated in the auditorium…and he could sit on the opposite side.

His odd behavior bothered him, but not as

much as the events at the toy store this afternoon. And throughout Brother Henry's lesson, his mind kept replaying that moment when he realized Emmie's choice of stuffed animals was a tribute to her mommy. And that Dee's toy choice...was a tribute to Kate.

By the time the Bible class ended, he'd glanced across the auditorium at least a dozen times at the woman who indeed resembled Dee's new Snow White figure. Something about her captivated him, and Mitch had no idea why. Nor did he like the reaction. He didn't want to be captivated. And as much as he wanted to deny it, he kind of hoped to catch her looking his way upon one of those glances. Didn't happen.

He turned and exited the auditorium to go get the girls and noticed a small group of church members moving toward the new lady for introductions. Probably a good thing. He could pick up Emmie and Dee from class, get home and get a grip on the bizarre twist of spiraling emotions—a combination of guilt, fear...and infatuation.

That last one was the kicker, because he couldn't deny that Dee's infatuation with the lady had nothing on Mitch's.

Lord, help me deal with this, he silently prayed as he went to the nursery to pick up

Emmie. *I can tell she's a good person, and I know I need her help in the office—that's what I asked You for, and You delivered—but I need help battling this pull toward her. You know I'm not ready for that, Lord, and I don't think my girls are ready for it, either. Help me out here, God, please.*

"Emmie seems to be feeling better," Annette Tingle said, handing her over to Mitch. Mrs. Tingle worked in the nursery on Wednesday evenings. Mitch liked knowing the sweet lady was watching after his little girl. As his neighbor, she'd been around the girls almost daily since they were born and consequently treated them like granddaughters. "Tell Daddy who we talked about tonight, Emmie."

Emmie grinned. "Je-sus."

Mitch nodded, always happy to see the girls learning about their Lord while so young. "That's great, Emmie. You can't go wrong there."

Mrs. Tingle reached for Emmie's diaper bag, hanging on a peg near the door. Usually the pegs were all filled, but tonight only one more bag was present. "Only had three in here tonight," she said. "Most of the town must be taking their summer vacations. Didn't seem to be as many in the auditorium, either, from what I could tell."

"Yeah, the attendance was low, but it'll pick back up in the next week or two. Bo and Maura do the big family vacation in May each year, too," he said, referring to his in-laws. "They are out of town until Sunday evening, and Matt, Hannah and Autumn are with them."

"Autumn," Emmie repeated.

Mitch realized he probably shouldn't have mentioned Autumn's name until his in-laws returned to town, because now Emmie peered over his shoulder and down the hall to see if she could spot her cousin. At eight years old, Autumn was the perfect age to play with Dee and Emmie as a "big girl," and they both adored her. "Autumn will be back in a few days," he said to Emmie.

Her lip poked out, but she recovered quickly when Mrs. Tingle handed her the stuffed bulldog that she'd left on the class table. "You don't want to forget your puppy," she said.

"Doggy!" Emmie snuggled the toy like she'd been doing all afternoon.

"No, we wouldn't want to forget that," Mitch agreed, still awed that she'd selected that particular animal.

Annette smiled then cleared her throat. "Kate told me this afternoon that she planned to come to church tonight."

Mitch zipped the top of the diaper bag. "Yes, she's here."

Annette waited, as though wanting him to say more. Mitch didn't, so she did.

"I'm so happy she came to town, aren't you? You've been needing help at the office, and she's good with the girls, too, isn't she?"

Mitch really didn't want to talk about this right now. He had a feeling half the town was already set to watch his interaction with Kate and determine whether their relationship could be leaning toward the personal. And he'd met her only two days ago. That was the thing about living in such a small town. Everyone knew everything about pretty much everyone. Sometimes that was a good thing; sometimes not so much. Like now. "I think she's going to be a good employee," he said, giving no enthusiasm, no emotion. Just stating the facts.

Mrs. Tingle lifted a brow. "Mmm-hmm," she said, as though she had more to say but chose not to, which was perfectly fine with Mitch.

"Thanks for taking care of Emmie," he said on his way to get Dee from her class. The classroom for three-and four-year-olds was located down the next hall. Mitch rounded the corner and saw Kate standing a short distance from

Dee's classroom door and staring at the bulletin board.

"Kay-Kay," Emmie said, pointing and smiling as they neared.

Mitch couldn't very well step past her without speaking; that'd just make this whole whatever-it-was more awkward, so he nodded toward the bulletin board decorated for spring and said, "About time for my sister-in-law to swap the theme to summer."

Kate jumped, apparently so absorbed in the collection of crepe paper flowers and trees that she hadn't heard them approach.

"Sorry, I didn't mean to startle you," Mitch said. He noticed that her face was tense, almost as though she were in pain. Her eyes were slightly red and tearstains lined her cheeks.

She coughed and covered her mouth with the action, then attempted to casually run her palm across one cheek to wipe away the evidence of those tears. "Your sister-in-law?" she finally managed to say.

"Jana's sister," he said, deciding it best not to bring up the fact that she'd been staring at a classroom bulletin board and crying. That might open up something that he didn't have any business knowing, and might possibly make him feel an even stronger connection toward the lady. He didn't need their connection to be any stronger. "Before Hannah married Dr. Graham she was a window designer on the square and decorated the storefronts for each of the merchants. Now she's a stay-at-home mom to their little girl, but she still likes to use her artistic talents whenever she can, and decorating the church bulletin boards is right up her alley."

Kate nodded. "It's going to take me a while to learn people's names and all of the relationships in town." She looked from Mitch back to the bulletin board. "But I do want to meet everyone and get to know them."

"Well, most folks will start coming back from their vacations soon, and with a town this size, it won't take you long before you're on a first-name basis with them all."

Kate nodded but didn't say anything.

"Sissie," Emmie said, pointing to Dee's picture, centering a bright yellow flower on the board. Each flower had a child's photo forming the middle, with crepe paper surrounding every smiling face.

"Yes, we need to pick up Sissie from class." Mitch thought about asking if Kate wanted to see the room, or see Dee, period, but then remembered Dee's choice of toys today and decided he shouldn't encourage his daughter's adoration. So he didn't say anything else before entering Dee's room.

"Everybody's gone," Dee said when she saw them entering. She gathered several take-home pages from the table, as well as a handmade finger puppet that must have been her craft for the night. "This is Joseph, but I'm the only one who made him."

Her teacher, Rossi Lankford, pointed to a stack of colorful fabric swatches on the table. "I wasn't thinking about all of the folks who would be out on vacation this week," she said. "So we have a lot of supplies left over for our Joseph puppets. I told Dee that we'd probably talk about him and his brothers again next week so that her friends can make a puppet, too."

"And I said that's okay, 'cause then I'll have two puppets," Dee said.

"That's right," Rossi agreed. "And we still had fun tonight even if it was just us, didn't we?"

"Yes, ma'am," Dee answered. "Hey, Daddy, where's Miss Kate? I want to show her my puppet."

Emmie had been absorbed in petting her bulldog, but she looked up and then pointed to the hall. "Kay-Kay."

"She's out there?" Dee asked, hurrying to the

door and out into the hall. "Where? I want her to see my class. Miss Kate! You here?"

Mitch thanked Rossi and then followed Dee into the hallway. He hadn't been in the classroom but a few minutes and had expected to run into Kate again when they exited, but she was gone.

"Kay-Kay?" Emmie looked toward the spot where Kate had been standing near the bulletin board.

"She must have left," Mitch said.

"Aww, I wanted to see her," Dee said.

Mitch didn't comment, but if he were being completely honest, he'd have to admit that he wanted to see her again, too.

Kate sat on one of the wooden rockers that lined the front porch of the B and B and stared at the full moon glowing prominently and spotlighting Mitch Gillespie's home across the street. She'd briefly spoken with the Tingles and a few of the other guests when she'd arrived home from church, but then she'd found sanctuary on the porch and was glad none of the other guests had decided to sit out here tonight. She needed to think, and she needed to pray.

God, that was so hard tonight. You knew it would be, but obviously You wanted me to go to that church, to hear that lesson on redemption and then to see that picture. You know I'm feeling weak, Lord, and I need strength. I need strength from You. Be with me over the next few weeks, and be with me when I go back for my checkup next week. Let everything be good again, God. And help me to say and do the right thing here. People aren't as willing to forgive as You are, but I pray that You will help them forgive me when they learn who I am.

The light in one of the upstairs windows at Mitch's home came on for a few minutes and then went off again, replaced by a more faint illumination. Kate suspected that Mitch had just put the girls to bed, probably said nighttime prayers and maybe read a story, and then turned their night-light on.

She wondered if Lainey slept with a night-light. Or a stuffed animal, like Emmie's bulldog. Did she say prayers? Did she pray for her mommy? Kate winced. Well, of course she did, but the mommy she prayed for certainly wasn't Kate.

Ever since they left the toy store this afternoon, Kate hadn't stopped thinking about Emmie's choice of that bulldog. Mr. Feazell's words echoed through her thoughts the rest of the day, especially when she'd gone to the church.

"They always say kids take after their parents in what they like and all."

Did Lainey take after Kate with the things that she liked? What *did* she like? What foods were her favorites? What types of toys would she pick out in the toy store? Did she talk a lot, like Dee? Or was she quiet and reserved, the way Kate had always been as a child?

Then again, Kate was usually quiet because she was sad. Her primary memories of childhood, after all, were of doing the wrong thing, saying the wrong thing, listening to her father and stepmom fighting. Laughter, particularly the kind of giggles and smiles that she'd seen from Dee and Emmie this afternoon, didn't exist in Kate's childhood.

She prayed it existed in Lainey's.

Mitch's screen door creaked as it opened, the sound carrying across the street to draw her attention to the man exiting his home.

Kate had been rocking steadily, but she paused the rocker and watched him make his way toward the mailbox by the street. He was tall, at least a couple of inches taller than Harrison Tinsdale, her ex, and he had a strong, confident presence about him when he moved. Kate assumed that was due to the responsibility of running a business, taking care of two little girls and dealing with the loss of his wife at such a young age. He'd become a single parent and a widower essentially overnight, and yet he seemed to handle it all okay.

Thankful for the depth of the porch hiding her in the shadows, Kate took advantage of the opportunity to observe the man she already admired.

Apparently, the entire town had one mailman, and Maple Street was at the end of his route, because the guy had been leaving mail in the boxes as Kate arrived at the B and B after church. She was thankful for that late delivery now, because it gave her the chance to see Mitch.

He retrieved the mail from the box and then stood there for a moment before starting back to the house. Kate watched his shoulders lift and fall, and then he took a hand to his forehead and appeared to squeeze his temples.

Maybe he wasn't handling it okay after all.

A cool evening breeze caused several pink petals to fall like snow from the branches of the cherry trees lining the street. They caught the moonlight and shimmered in Kate's path, the scent of the blossoms adding to the serenity of the night. But the man slowly making his way back to his house undoubtedly wasn't feeling the peacefulness, and truthfully neither was Kate.

She stood and, before she could change her mind, began walking toward her new boss. By the time she reached him, he'd paused at the top porch step, and Kate heard him exhale thickly in a deep sigh. "Mitch?"

Obviously surprised, he turned and tilted his head toward Kate. "I—didn't hear you come up," he said, then asked, "Everything okay, Kate? It's kind of late."

She felt strange now for walking over at this hour without an inkling of what she was going to say or do once she got here. "I was on the front porch enjoying the night, and I saw you walk out," she said, her voice trembling a bit due to her nerves. "And, well, you looked like something was wrong. I guess I wanted to see if I could help."

Even though he was only illuminated by moonlight, Kate still saw his eyes widen in surprise, and then she saw his head shake slightly and heard him mumble, "You really are a Snow White."

"Pardon?" She knew what he'd said but wasn't quite sure why he'd said it.

"Never mind." He breathed thickly again and added, "There is something wrong, and it has to do with you. I guess now's as good a time as any to apologize."

Not what she'd expected. "About me? Apologize for what?"

He motioned toward the oak swing hanging at one end of the porch. "Come on. We might as well sit down while I explain."

"Okay," she said slowly, and followed him to sit on the wooden swing. The breeze caused her to shiver, or maybe it was the fact that she was sitting this near to Mitch, so close in fact that she could sense his warmth, and she considered scooting closer to ward off the chill.

Not a good idea. She shifted a little, so that she sat farther from her boss.

The silence and the aloneness of this situation made Kate feel awkward. If she waited long enough, he would tell her what he wanted to talk about. But the quiet unnerved her, and she decided to end it. "It's nice out tonight," she said.

The swing creaked as he turned to face Kate. She'd kind of hoped this conversation would occur with the two of them looking straight ahead, across the porch and toward the towering cherry trees, so she focused on the bloom-covered branches swaying in the breeze, several of those delicate pink petals catching the wind and putting on a mesmerizing show as they tumbled to the ground.

"Kate, I want to talk to you for a second. This

is hard for me, but I need to do it, and I'd like for you to look at me when I do, if you don't mind."

His voice was so solemn, so serious, that she had no choice but to turn and face him, his face appearing even more grim within the gray shadow of the porch. Kate ached for him. She had no idea what had caused this disposition, but his earlier comment signified that it had something to do with her. Had he figured out who she really was? That she'd hurt one of his best friends? And if that was it, why would he need to apologize?

"I didn't treat you right this evening," he said, "at church."

She quickly replayed the earlier events, from the time she'd followed him to the church to his introduction to the preacher to the Bible lesson—when they hadn't even been sitting near each other, so that couldn't have been it—to the time he'd seen her in the class hallway. Not once did she remember him treating her badly. "You treated me fine," she said.

"No." He shook his head. "I didn't. And if you didn't notice it, well, then, I guess you aren't used to true Southern hospitality, but I am. That's who I am, and where I come from, and tonight I tossed it in the trash and ignored you."

"Ignored me," she repeated, having no idea when he'd ignored her.

"I could have directed you to a class. I could have introduced you to more church members, other than just Brother Henry when we walked in. And I could have spoken to you instead of merely stepping past you in the hall—" he paused "—as if you aren't important." He ran a hand through his hair. "You are important. Even though you've only been here a few days, you're already making a difference at my office, and I guess in my life. Mine and the girls' lives. And that's, I suppose, why I ignored you. But it isn't right for me to treat you badly just because I'm feeling guilty."

Kate used to get confused every now and then when she was taking the radiation and the chemo. Her thoughts would get muddled, and she couldn't wrap her mind around sentences to find the meaning. That was how she felt now, and she didn't like it, at all. But she also couldn't make heads or tails of what he'd "explained." So she asked, "Mitch, I don't understand. You said you treated me badly—which I will disagree with from the get-go, by the way—and you did it because you felt guilty. Guilty about what?"

His jaw tensed, and he ran his hand through his hair another time, causing it to stand on end.

He certainly didn't care. "You may not have even noticed it this afternoon, but I did. The people around town, when they saw us together, I believe some of them, probably most of them, saw us as…" He hesitated, then plunged ahead. "They saw us as a potential couple."

Kate had picked up on a hint of that from Mr. Feazell at the toy store, but she'd also thought he'd figured out the truth before they left. "I think once you explained that I am your employee, they knew that we weren't." Then realization dawned. "But you felt guilty," she whispered, "because you felt like you were betraying your wife's memory? Because they *assumed* you might be interested in someone else?"

He nodded, and Kate's heart skipped in her chest. He'd loved his wife so much that even a year and a half after she'd passed away, he felt guilty for even presenting the assumption that he was seeing someone else. What kind of love was that?

"Oh, Mitch, I'm so sorry. I will take extra care not to give off the wrong impression of our relationship." She leaned toward him as she spoke now, wanting him to know that she meant every word and was no longer uncomfortable facing him straight on. She didn't want to hide from him. She wanted to get to know more about this compelling man who, with every action and every word, reinforced the fact that he was a good man, faithful and honest, who worked hard at his job, loved his God and his little girls…and still loved their mother so much that he didn't want to mar her memory with ru- s of a new female interest. "It may be my that they got the wrong idea," she said.

e shook his head. "I don't understand how ld be your fault, Kate."

ecause I—" She debated how much to say. asn't certain how he'd handle the truth who she was and what she'd done, but she felt he deserved to know why she was so drawn to him now. And maybe that was what the shop owners had picked up on, her awe toward this man.

"Because you what, Kate?" he asked, obviously anxious to hear the rest of her confession.

Kate decided to tell him the truth. Some of it, anyway. And pray that God would forgive her— and that Mitch would forgive her—for not giving him everything yet. She just wasn't ready.

"They may have gotten the wrong idea because I admire you so much. I'm captivated by you, truthfully. Maybe they saw that, and maybe they got the wrong idea about why."

His mouth opened, and then he closed it before he said...whatever had come to mind. Kate wished he'd have blurted it out; that was what she'd just done. Turnabout was fair play, after all, and then maybe she wouldn't feel so exposed now, as though someone had yanked a bandage off her heart.

Finally, he said, "You just met me three days ago. How could you be—" he grimaced as though he found it hard to say the next word, then continued "—*captivated* by me?"

"Because you've done it all right. What I wish I'd have done from the start, and what I would love to go back and do over, but I can't. You accepted responsibility and you found the courage to give Dee and Emmie every bit of your life and your love. You're a real parent—" tears burned as they pushed forward "—and that's what I so wish I could be."

"You want to be a mother," he said softly, as though he understood.

But he didn't. "I had a daughter," she said, "nearly four years ago." She blinked through more tears. "She's the same age as Dee."

"You *had* a daughter?" he asked, his voice tender with emotion. "What happened, Kate?"

"I gave her up." Her chin trembled, and a sucking gasp escaped. "Seeing you, watching how wonderful you are with Dee and Emmie—" another loud, un-ladylike sniff "—is why I'm so captivated with you. Because you're everything that I wasn't. I—gave—her—up."

Her sobs tore through the stillness of the night, but they were soon smothered against the broad planes of Mitch's chest, because he pulled her close, holding her through the pain, through the tears and whispering the words he must've thought she wanted to hear.

"I'm so sorry, Kate. It'll be okay. Everything will be okay."

But Kate thought of that bulletin board at the church and Lainey's sweet, beautiful face smiling at her from the center of that yellow crepe paper flower, and her tears fell harder, because she knew that, when the entire truth came out, everything would definitely not be okay.

Chapter Six

"You wait here, Daddy," Dee instructed. "I want to get Miss Kate by myself."

Mitch admired the independent spirit growing stronger and stronger in his oldest princess, a quality she'd undoubtedly inherited from Jana. His late wife had been "strong-willed," as her family called it, finding it difficult to ask for help and thrilling to accomplish any task on her own. Dee was a pint-size version of the woman he'd loved, and he thanked God for reminding him this week—with Emmie's selection of the stuffed bulldog she currently clutched in her arms and with Dee's determination now to get Miss Kate by herself—that Jana would always be here, a part of their lives, in spirit.

Following Dee's request that he stay put, Mitch stood his ground near the towering magnolia that filled one side of the bed-and-breakfast's front yard. When Dee teetered a little on the third step, he moved forward.

"I'm okay," she said quickly.

"I know you are," he said, never wanting to stifle that independence, "but it'll be easier if you let me hold the bread or Snow White so you can use the rails."

She had her treasured Snow White figurine in one hand and a bag of bread in the other. She'd insisted she could carry both—and she could—but hauling them while also tackling the B and B's stairs wasn't so easy. He took another step toward her, but she shook her red pigtails. "I can do it," she said, and then moved the Disney figure to the opposite hand so that she grasped both the knotted bread bag and the prized princess in her left fist. "See?" she asked excitedly, putting her other hand on the rail and continuing toward the door.

Amazing, the pride he felt at watching her figure things out on her own. "Yes," he said, "I do see, and you're doing a great job."

Emmie wiggled in his arms so she could watch her big sister complete her way up the steps, across the porch and to the front door. "Kay-Kay," she said, obviously looking forward to seeing Kate today as much as Dee.

And as much as Mitch.

For the past three days, ever since their conversation late Wednesday evening, he hadn't stopped thinking about the petite, black-haired beauty that had fallen apart in his arms. He'd wanted to protect her that night; in fact, he'd wanted to protect her ever since. She'd admitted something so personal—that she'd given up a child—and Mitch had felt her pain so intensely that he'd gone to bed that night wiping away his own tears.

He couldn't imagine giving up a child, couldn't imagine a life that didn't include his precious Dee or Emmie. And even though he didn't know the details about why Kate had chosen to give up her baby, he knew the end result. She ached for a child she never knew.

And maybe because of that, she'd quickly grown to adore Mitch's children. He could see her affection toward Dee and Emmie every time she spoke to them, looked at them. And he sensed that God had brought Kate Wydell to Claremont for more than merely providing Mitch with someone to help him at the office. He'd brought her here because He didn't merely plan on Kate helping Mitch; He planned on Mitch helping Kate.

Bonding with Dee and Emmie provided a salve for her soul, and he realized that their growing relationship with Kate was something he shouldn't fight or feel guilty about. This was good for his girls, good for Kate...and maybe even good for Mitch.

He enjoyed the journey raising the girls. And, though it took him a few days to adjust to the idea, he also enjoyed the fact that Kate was becoming a part of their lives. They had their grandmother, their aunt Hannah and their teachers at school and day care, so it wasn't as if they hadn't been around adult females before, but there was something different about the way they were around Kate.

And the way Kate was around his girls. Even though she'd known them only a week, he was certain that every time she looked at Dee and Emmie, he saw love.

Kate must have seen them coming, because the door opened to reveal the object of his thoughts standing on the other side.

"Well, hey," she said, her smile beaming at Dee. She wore a red sundress similar to the blue one she'd worn earlier in the week, the skirt skimming her ankles, except she didn't have the jacket on this time, and Mitch's attention was drawn to her slender neck and shoulders. A small gold locket rested beneath her throat, and it glistened in the morning sunlight. Although he'd been around her every day this week, Mitch still found himself momentarily taken hostage by her beauty. She didn't seem to be aware of the effect on him, which was good.

"Is it time to go now?" she asked Dee.

"We got old bread." Dee lifted the half loaf of wheat bread, smashed to smithereens from her desire to carry it on her own. She'd dropped it a couple of times before they'd even made it out of the house and then had swung it like a lopsided purse ever since.

"I see that." Kate managed to keep her smile in place without so much as a giggle at the pitiful bag of bread. "Do you know what?"

"What?" Dee asked.

Emmie, wanting to join in on the conversation, said, "Wha?"

Kate laughed. "I told Mrs. Tingle that we were going to feed the ducks today, and she gave us all of her leftover bread from breakfast."

"How much?" Dee asked, leaning to the side to peer past Kate.

Kate crooked her finger, grinned at Mitch and Emmie and then steered Dee inside. A few seconds later, Dee dashed out with both hands clutching grocery bags that each held at least two loaves of bread. "Look at this, Daddy!" She held up her prize.

"Wow!" Mitch exclaimed. "That sure is a lot of bread. What did you do with the loaf you had?"

"Miss Kate put it in here. She said I could carry these by myself. And we put Snow White in my pocket." She glanced down to her chest, where the figure's dark head peeked over the pocket of her pink shirt.

Her smile stretched into both cheeks, and Mitch knew he hadn't made a bad decision inviting Kate on their outing today. They'd worked hard all week, first at Mitch's home—while taking care of sick children, no less—and then at the office. They deserved a day of fun, and he knew Kate would enjoy it more if Dee and Emmie were a part of the activities. Feeding the ducks seemed perfect. Nothing too intimate that would suggest a date to prying eyes, but private enough that they could enjoy the gorgeous day and the girls without a huge crowd. There would be some people at Hydrangea Park, no doubt, but the place was large enough that he, Kate and the girls could find a spot for feeding the ducks.

"I've actually got a few things for us to bring," Kate said, carrying an oversize picnic basket.

Annette Tingle followed Kate onto the porch. "Kate told me y'all were going to Hydrangea

Park to feed the ducks, and the day is so pretty that I thought it might be nice if you had a picnic while you're there. I surprised her by packing y'all a basket."

"A picnic! Yay!" Dee looked to Mitch. "You hear that, Daddy? We're gonna have a picnic!"

"I heard," he said. A picnic. Feeding the ducks had seemed like a fun activity, definitely nowhere near the date realm. A picnic in the park *and* feeding the ducks…teetered on the edge of *date* classification. Then again, was it considered a date if you brought your children along? Maybe that fact kept this situation clear, and it eased Mitch's concern for folks getting the wrong idea again.

"And I've got a little surprise, too," Kate said. "Let me put this basket in the car and I'll go get it."

Mitch shifted Emmie to his left hip and moved toward Kate. "Here, I'll take the basket for you."

Their hands brushed as he claimed the wooden handle, and the hint of peaches that always surrounded Kate caused him to inhale deeper; however, that scent was quickly overpowered by the smells escaping that basket. "Fried chicken?" he asked.

"I thought the girls would like chicken tenders," Annette said, "and I also put in some homemade potato salad, baked beans and coleslaw. Oh, and a few fried apple pies. They were still hot from the oven, so I added a little silver shaker of powdered sugar for you to put on top before you eat them. That makes them taste better, you know."

Mitch wasn't hungry, but his stomach growled anyway, and Mrs. Tingle grinned.

"Sounds like you're gonna enjoy them," she said.

"I can't imagine anyone not enjoying all of that," he said honestly, thinking that the picnic wasn't a bad idea after all. He couldn't remember the last time he'd been on a picnic or had that kind of home-cooked food. Oh, wait, earlier this week he had, and courtesy of the same sweet neighbor. "Thanks, Mrs. Tingle. I really appreciate this."

"I do, too," Kate said, and then she hugged Annette, but it wasn't a typical thank-you type hug. She held her for a moment, gently squeezing her close. "You've been so good to me."

Mrs. Tingle sniffed then blinked a couple of times. "Oh, child, you touch my heart." Then she broke the hug and gave Kate a tender smile. "Now you go enjoy yourself today. Everything's going to be just fine."

Mitch wondered what the woman referred to. Had Kate also told her about the child she'd given up? Had she told the lady that she was "captivated," as she put it, by Mitch's parenting of his girls? Or was there more currently bonding Mrs. Tingle to Kate?

He shouldn't feel he needed to know. Kate was his employee, and he knew as much as he should know about an employee. But they'd moved beyond employee status Wednesday night when he'd held her in his arms. Friends, maybe? Or perhaps *comforters* would be a better term.

Had Kate gotten upset again, needed someone for comfort and turned to Mrs. Tingle?

And if she did, Mitch wondered...why her? And why not him?

"You said you have a surprise," Dee reminded Kate, then gave her a full baby-teeth grin. "What is it?"

"I'll go get it," Kate said, turning and darting back into the house.

Mitch opened the trunk of his car with the key fob and then walked toward it to put the basket inside and to get his mind off whether or not Kate had confided in Mrs. Tingle instead of him. Dee's squeal of delight forced him to look back to the porch, where Kate had exited with a kite in each hand, one bright yellow with a smiley in the center, the other bright pink with the same smiley.

"Daddy, look!" Dee yelled.

"Wook!" Emmie repeated.

Kate and Dee hurried toward the car, Dee swinging the bread bags as she'd been doing all day, but now with a little extra jump in her step, and Kate laughing softly.

"I went to the toy store as soon as it opened this morning to see if Mr. Feazell had any kites, and he did!" Kate said excitedly. "He said the wind should be just right for kite flying. Won't it be fun to fly them in the park?"

"Yes!" Dee said, flinging her bread bags into the trunk so hard that Snow White fell out of her pocket. She hurried to pick her up and then rubbed her clean on the bottom of her shirt.

"Fun!" Emmie raised her tiny shoulders and clapped her hands together. "Kay-Kay! Fun!"

Mitch nodded. She was right. Kay-Kay was planning to have fun with the girls today, and he should be happy about that. He shouldn't be wondering why she'd talked to someone else instead of him. That'd be the type of thing someone with a personal interest in her would do, and he didn't have a personal interest.

And even if he ever did, she didn't feel that

way about him. She'd said she was captivated, but because of his parenting, not because of Mitch himself.

"Let's go have some fun," he said, and he resolved to do just that.

After putting the girls in their car seats and then waiting for Kate to climb in (and bring along that peach scent he'd grown accustomed to), they backed out of the driveway and waved goodbye to Mrs. Tingle, still standing on the porch.

She waved back, and then she clasped her hands together beneath her lips while she watched them drive away.

Mitch got the strangest sensation that the woman was praying.

Kate laughed as the pink kite tilted to the right and then circled back to the left, the wind catching it and sliding it through the sky while the baby in her arms giggled.

"Pretty!" Emmie said and then bestowed an openmouthed, wet, sloppy kiss on Kate's cheek.

"Oh, Emmie, thank you," Kate said, snuggling her close as they cheered on their kite.

"Ours is higher, Miss Kate!" Dee yelled from where she stood holding the spindle of string.

"Yes, it is, isn't it? You're really good at this,

Dee," Kate said, and she watched as Dee tilted her head to rest on her daddy's shoulder and grinned, her eyes never leaving the yellow smiling kite.

Mitch knelt beside Dee with his arms around hers to help her maintain control of the cord as their kite slowly but surely made its way closer and closer to the clouds. He kissed Dee's forehead. "Love you, sweetie," he said.

"Love you, Daddy," she answered, and Kate's heart melted.

Just two weeks ago, she'd attended the Mother's Day service at her church in Atlanta, watched the smiling faces of moms and children displayed in the slide-show presentation before the sermon and wept for everything she'd lost. She'd cried because she'd thought she might never get to experience moments like this.

"Kay-Kay," Emmie said, and then gave her yet another of those wet kisses.

"You are too sweet," Kate said into that giggling, smiling face. "You know that?"

"Kay-Kay," Emmie repeated happily.

Kate snuggled her again and then heard the searing crack of a kite gone rogue. She jerked her attention upward and, sure enough, that pink smiley face jerked and heaved back and forth so much that Kate didn't know if it'd come crashing to the ground or pull itself free from the string completely and make a run for the ocean. "Oh, dear." She knew the little girl in her arms wouldn't be pleased if she saw that smiley disappear, and Kate didn't want any sadness associated with this day. They'd had so much fun feeding the ducks, eating their picnic lunch, pushing the girls on the swings and now flying their kites. Those were the things she wanted to remember from today, not watching Emmie's pretty kite float away.

But the thing was pulling into the wind so hard now that the spindle had started spinning too fast for Kate to regain control, or at least to regain control with a baby in her arms.

"No!" Emmie yelled, pointing to the pink smile now slashing across the sky like a pen trying to write a name in the clouds. A messy name.

"I'm trying to stop it," Kate said. She heard Mitch instruct Dee on holding her spindle secure until he returned. Where was he going?

And then she knew, because his arms wrapped around hers the way they'd been wrapped around Dee's a moment ago. She felt the warmth of his chest against her back.

"I'll help you," he said against her left ear,

and then his lips brushed her cheek as he told Emmie, "Daddy will get it, sweetie."

Every inch of Kate's skin tingled as he capably manipulated the spindle, working the string in and out until he regained control, his biceps flexing against Kate's arms with every maneuver, and Kate's heart thundering so hard that she was certain it'd knocked against her ribs. Until this moment, she'd thought of this day as a family day, the type of day she'd have if she could be a real mother. Except now she realized that in her true dreams, there was a man in the picture. A loving daddy and husband who would come to their rescue, be strong and capable, gain control of every situation. A man she could love and honor and trust and be faithful to for as long as she lived.

A man like Mitch.

"Okay, I think you're good now," he said, the warmth of his words feathering across her left ear and trickling down her neck, and then he eased his hands away from hers—have mercy, she'd been so lost in the close proximity, she hadn't realized his hands had covered hers completely—and he tenderly touched Emmie's soft curls. "Everything's better now," he said.

"Daddy," Emmie said sweetly.

"That's my girl." He smiled at them before

moving back toward Dee, and Kate fought to keep her shaky knees from allowing her to collapse to the ground.

Then, in spite of the fact that she had to keep her attention on the kite and the spindle so that she could keep the thing harnessed, she shot an occasional glance at her boss, kneeling again next to his little girl and guiding her as she steadily worked the string and allowed her kite to soar even higher.

"I love you, Daddy," Dee said.

"Love you, too," he answered.

Kate swallowed thickly. That was what this day was filled with more than anything else—love. She hadn't been around it in so long… maybe ever. And the realization slammed her, as did the realization that it wouldn't be that hard…to fall in love with Mitch.

Chapter Seven

Kate checked her email in-box again. Nothing new there. She scanned the checklist on her computer for all of the tasks she had to complete before the day ended. They were all done. Then she looked back to her in-box once more. Still empty. So at only four-thirty in the afternoon, all of her work was done. She'd made a list for tomorrow, but she really didn't want to get started and then be in the middle of a policy when it was time to go home at five o'clock, not that she was heading straight to the B and B today.

She'd decided to drive to the Stockville Community College and talk to Chad. Today would be his first day back after vacation. Maybe her nerves about finally telling him she'd returned and that she wanted to see Lainey were what sent her adrenaline pumping and caused her to work so feverishly that she'd finished early.

She looked up to see Mitch reading something on his computer, his hand resting against his chin and his index finger rubbing across his lower lip the way it always did when he was deep in thought. Kate had started learning his mannerisms. She'd also learned that his favorite meal from the local diner, where they'd had lunch today, was grilled chicken and steamed vegetables, followed by a splurge of homemade banana pudding. He'd encouraged her to also splurge, and she'd happily eaten every bite.

There were other things she'd learned over the past week about Mitch Gillespie. She knew he adored his little girls and sacrificed his own personal life in lieu of making sure they were happy. Or maybe he sacrificed his personal life because he still loved—and always would—his deceased wife.

Kate admired that kind of love.

She easily remembered his arms wrapped around *her* Saturday when he'd helped her with that kite. Easily, because she hadn't stopped thinking about that moment ever since. It'd felt so wonderful spending the day with him and the girls at the park, like a real family. And until he'd helped her regain control of that kite, she'd have said that all she felt that day was a sense of family. But then he'd held her—kind of—and Kate hadn't wanted him to let go. And after that moment, she'd found herself feeling more than the "family" setting; she'd gotten a brief glimpse of what having a loving husband would be like, and she'd been absorbed in *that* dream ever since.

A pang of regret shot to her heart. She'd *had* a loving husband. She'd *had* a beautiful baby girl. And she'd thrown them both away.

"Kate," Mitch said, looking up to find her still staring at him. She must not have disguised her sadness quickly enough because he tilted his head and asked, "You okay?"

She swallowed, blinked, nodded. "Yes, I just realized that I've finished everything I had on my list of things to do today, and I wasn't sure whether to start on the next policy." It wasn't a lie, exactly, because that was where her thoughts had started. It certainly wasn't where they'd ended, though, and the scrutiny in his gaze said he knew it. Even so, Kate wasn't ready to explain, so she continued, "Do you have something else I could work on for the next half hour?"

He shook his head. "No. Why don't you leave early? You've hardly come up for air today beyond taking the short break for lunch, so it doesn't surprise me that you finished."

"But I'm leaving early tomorrow, remember? I don't want to leave early two days in a row." She'd need to leave by two o'clock tomorrow to make her doctor's appointment in Atlanta, so she'd requested the afternoon off. Mitch had told her she could go, and he also hadn't asked her any specifics about her "appointment," which was good. She'd tell him about her past in due time—her past with Chad…and her past with chemo.

"Doesn't matter. We're ahead of schedule on pretty much everything, probably because I've never had any help and because you're so efficient." He grinned, and Kate was pretty sure she felt that smile to her toes. "Go on and head out. After I pick the girls up, maybe we can all get together if you want."

Kate returned the smile. That was exactly what she wanted. "That'd be great." The phone rang, and he reached for the one on his desk, but she shook her head. "No, I'll get it."

"I told you to head on out," he said, but Kate merely shrugged and answered.

"Gillespie Insurance Agency, this is Kate. How can I help you?"

"Um, I'm sorry. You did say Gillespie Insurance Agency, right?" the woman stammered. "I dialed the right number?"

"Yes." Kate switched windows on her computer to bring up the main page for accounts. "How can I help you?"

"And you said your name is Kate?" she asked.

Kate heard another woman's voice in the background. "Kate? Who's Kate? Do you know any Kates in town? I don't. Wait, she works there? With Mitch?"

The woman on the line whispered, "I'll find out, Maura. Let me ask."

Kate remembered Mitch mentioning that Maura was his mother-in-law, so she now knew who the person in the background was, and she suspected the identity of the woman speaking. Hannah. Mitch's sister-in-law. Unlike most everyone else in town, Kate knew the face that went with the voice because Hannah Graham—Hannah Taylor at the time—had been on the welcome committee at the Claremont Community Church and had brought a meal to Chad and Kate when they first arrived in Claremont. She was very pretty, like her sister, Jana, Mitch's wife. Kate, of course, had never stepped foot in the church before she left town. But she remembered how extremely friendly and welcoming Hannah had been toward her back then. Would she be so friendly if she put two and two together and realized who was on the line? And would she recognize Kate now?

The lady cleared her throat. "Kate, um, well, hi. I'm Hannah Graham. I'm Mitch's…" She stalled a moment, so Kate answered.

"Oh, yes, you're his sister-in-law. He's told me about you," Kate said, determined to keep the conversation flowing smoothly and not show any sign that she knew exactly who the woman was. "How was your vacation?"

"Well, it was fine, but—he told you about me? I'm sorry, but we didn't know Mitch had hired anyone. And I don't think we've met."

"I just moved to Claremont last week and answered his ad in the paper for an office manager." Kate glanced up to find Mitch's eyes locked on her.

"They're wondering what's up," he whispered loud enough for Kate to hear but quiet enough that Hannah didn't. "Better let me talk to her."

"I'll transfer you to Mitch," she said, and then flinched at her casual use of his first name. No doubt his sister-in-law would notice and probably get the wrong idea. "Mr. Gillespie," she corrected.

"Okay," Hannah said, drawing out the word. Kate hit the transfer button and then nodded toward Mitch, who had a soft smile playing on his lips.

Goose bumps trickled down Kate's arms at that smile.

"Hi, Hannah. Hold on just a second, okay?" He cupped his hand over the phone. "You can go ahead and leave early, Kate. No problem."

She nodded, retrieved her purse from her desk drawer and then started out, but she didn't miss Mitch's next words.

"Yes, I finally hired someone, and she's a godsend, Hannah."

Kate continued to her car even though she'd have loved to have heard what else Mitch said to his sister-in-law. Did he really see her as a godsend? And did he mean for the office only, or for more?

After she talked to Chad today, she planned to tell Mitch the truth about who she was and why she'd come to Claremont. Would he still see her as a godsend then?

Mitch closed his computer down while he talked to Hannah. He knew their conversation would last a while and, like Kate, he'd completed all of today's tasks. In fact, for the past fifteen minutes he hadn't done any work at all, merely stared at his computer screen while remembering how good it had felt to be so close to her on Saturday. And knowing that he wanted to be that close to her again.

Something was changing in Mitch, and he suspected he knew what. He'd talked to people before who had lost their spouses and found it difficult to move on. Mitch hadn't thought he'd ever feel that sensation they had described when they said, "You will know when the time is right."

Apparently, the time was right, because in merely a week, he'd gone from guilt to infatuation to interest. A definite interest. But he wanted to take the time to examine his feelings, make sure he wasn't acting too impulsively and that he let the relationship develop in due time. Besides, he had a family to think about. Jana's family, his only family, since his parents had passed away in a car accident when Mitch was only twenty-two and he had no siblings. Jana's family had essentially adopted him and the girls, so it made sense that Hannah sounded concerned over his new hire. And probably the fact that she'd referred to him by his first name on the phone.

He smiled again, thinking of Kate's red cheeks when she'd realized the slip. She was cute all of the time, but she was *really* cute when she blushed.

"So she's new in town?" Hannah continued. "What brought her to Claremont?"

Mitch still wondered the same thing, and he hoped she'd tell him the truth eventually because he was certain he hadn't heard it yet. Even so, he told Hannah the same thing Kate told him. "She said she was tired of living in the big city and wanted to give small-town living a try."

"And she picked Claremont." It wasn't a question, but her surprise at the fact was evident in her tone.

"Yes, she did," he said. "Pretty lucky for me, with all of her office experience, let me tell you."

"Uh-huh."

Mitch could almost see Hannah lifting her shoulders in one of those I-don't-get-it moves to Maura, who was probably shaking her head and figuring out exactly how long it'd take her to meet this "Kate."

As if following Mitch's thoughts to the letter, Hannah then asked, "So I guess we'll come by your office tomorrow and meet her, welcome her to town and all."

Mitch smirked. *Check her out and make sure she's okay to be around your brother-in-law and nieces is more like it.* But he answered, "That'd be fine."

"Oh, and, Mitch, I almost forgot the main reason I called," she said.

"What's that?"

"Muffins with Mom at the day care," she said. "I know I told you that Autumn and I would go with the girls on Friday, but I forgot that I have a doctor's appointment that morning."

Last year Hannah and Autumn had spent the morning at the day care, and Dee and Emmie hadn't seemed to notice any difference from the other children who had their mommies with them for the special day. Muffins with Mom was a celebration the day care had every May to coincide with the month for Mother's Day, and Doughnuts with Dad followed in the month of June to coincide with Father's Day. Mitch had loved sharing the breakfast treat with his girls on "his" day, almost as much as he'd hated the thought of them not having their mom with them for what would have been "her" special day.

"Maura is going to keep Autumn for me while I go to my appointment, though," Hannah continued, "and so we thought she could go to the day care and take Autumn along, too. I think the girls would enjoy that, don't you?"

Relief flooded through him, and Mitch thanked God for Hannah and Maura, watching out for him and Dee and Emmie as always. "Yes, I think they'd enjoy that a lot," he said.

"We do, too. And again, I'm sorry I told you I could go and now have to bail. It's my annual screening," she said.

"That's important." Mitch knew how important because those screenings were what detected whether cancer had returned. Hannah was a breast-cancer survivor. Mitch still remembered the pain of learning that Jana's cancer had returned during her pregnancy with Emmie. He'd prayed and prayed, but God had determined it was her time to go, and Mitch had determined to somehow continue living.

"I knew you would understand," Hannah said. "It's not smart to reschedule, in case, well, you know."

Mitch nodded. He knew how important it was to find the cancer early and to treat it promptly. He also knew what would happen if you ignored the treatment, say, for fear of hurting your child. He thought of Jana, and then of Emmie. "It's fine, Hannah. Really. I hope everything goes well with your appointment."

"Thanks, Mitch. We'll see you soon."

She disconnected, and Mitch found himself

looking to the desk across the office and its empty chair. Kate had asked to leave early tomorrow for a doctor's appointment, but she'd never said what kind. He suddenly wondered whether she would be going through a screening, too.

No, it was probably an annual female exam, or something else that would cause her to simply say she had an "appointment" without explanation. There was no reason at all for him to think it was anything more. Kate would have told him if it were serious. Surely, she would. Mitch knew he was starting to feel *something* toward the dark-haired beauty, and he also knew his heart couldn't handle watching someone he cared about deal with that horrid disease again. No way, no how.

Kate parked her car in a visitor spot at the Stockville Community College, gathered her courage and said a fervent prayer that Chad would forgive her. Had it been only three years ago when Chad left his med-school dreams behind in Atlanta and took the job as a professor in the biology department here in an effort to save their marriage?

Hard to believe how much had happened in

those three years. Hard to believe how much Kate had changed.

Would Chad believe it? And would it change the way Mitch felt about her when he realized she was "Chad's Kate"?

The breeze that had been consistent lately and had helped them fly those kites on Saturday picked up again as she walked across the quad and toward the sciences building. It pushed against her face as she moved, and it forced her eyes to water.

Or maybe she'd simply started to cry and wanted to blame it on the wind.

Kate reached the building and paused before starting inside.

God, be with me now. And, Lord, please be with Chad. Give him a forgiving heart, and give me the strength to get through this. And, God, if it be Your will, let me have a chance with my little girl.

"Here you go."

Kate looked up to see a boy who looked like he was barely eighteen holding the door open for her to enter the building. "Thank you," she said, and then asked, "Do you happen to know where Chad Martin's office is located?" She'd never even seen his office. Chad had brought her to the campus and shown her the sciences building when he'd decided to take the job, but she had hightailed it back to Atlanta so fast she'd never seen the actual office.

"Sure," the boy said with a grin. "Up the stairs to the second floor, last door on the right."

"Thanks." She entered the building and was surprised at the high ceilings with several inches of ornate crown molding, polished dark cherry accents on creamy white walls and white marble tiled floors. Chad had been so excited to get the position with "one of the oldest, most prestigious community colleges in the nation," as he'd described it. But Kate had heard the words *community college* and turned her nose in the air.

What a fool she'd been.

Several students met her in the stairwell and along the hallway as she made her way toward Chad's office. Most spoke cordially, and Kate attempted to answer even though her throat had started to tighten and her heart constricted in her chest. Three years ago, she didn't believe this place "big enough" for her, didn't believe Claremont "good enough" and didn't believe Chad Martin "man enough."

She'd spewed hateful words at the man who'd done nothing but love her as she packed her bags and started out the door. And then she'd spouted pure venom when she told him the truth about Lainey...and twisted the knife.

The wounded look on his face as she slammed the door was tattooed permanently on her mind and on her heart.

And yet she'd simply kept walking.

She stopped a few feet from Chad's door, uncertain whether she could enter. Her stomach lurched, and she regretted that she'd eaten lunch because she feared it was ready to make a reappearance.

Help me, God.

"You need help, miss?"

The deep baritone surprised her, as it seemed it might have come from God himself, hearing her cry and answering so loudly on her heart that she trembled. But she turned to see an older man smiling nearby.

"Are you looking for a particular class?" that same deep voice asked. "I'm the dean here. Maybe I can help."

"I—I'm here to see Mr. Martin," she said. "Chad Martin." She pointed toward the door bearing Chad's nameplate. "Just gathering my courage," she said honestly, without adding she was also fighting the urge to get sick.

"Well, you're at the right office, but Dr. Martin is on vacation. You can talk to his office assistant and set up an appointment for when he returns next week, though, if you'd like. Her name is Lynn, and she'll be happy to help you."

Kate took a small step back, the man's words hitting her as if he'd kicked her. She'd actually called the school and spoken with Chad's assistant two weeks ago, after Mother's Day and after she'd decided she didn't want another year to pass without knowing her little girl. She'd been told he was on vacation and assumed he'd be back this week. Obviously, his vacation was lasting longer than she'd anticipated. He'd be gone until next week?

"Are you okay?" The older man's concerned tone told Kate that she probably looked as bad as she felt.

"I'm actually not feeling well," she said, then spotted an antique wooden bench a short way down the hall and started walking toward it. "I'm going to sit down for a moment."

He walked beside her and then said, "I'll get you a cup of water."

Kate didn't have the wherewithal to stop him, and she also thought some water might help her queasiness. Within seconds, he returned holding a white cone-shaped cup filled with cold water that did indeed make her feel better. "Thank you," she said.

"You're welcome," he answered. "Is there anything else I can do for you?"

Make Chad come back sooner. Let me see my little girl. Help me get my life back on track. There were several things—important things—Kate needed, but nothing that she could obtain from this man. "No, but thank you for your kindness."

He nodded. "Well, I'm sure Dr. Martin will be happy to speak to you once he returns." Then he gave her another smile and walked away.

Dr. Martin. Doctor.

She hadn't realized he'd obtained his doctorate, and the irony of the fact broadsided her. She'd been so angry when he dropped out of med school, because she'd wanted to be married to a doctor. But he'd quit because she'd been so unhappy about the hours he spent in school and studying; he'd wanted to save the marriage. He hadn't even realized that, in Kate's heart, the marriage was already over.

Now, although it wasn't in the medical field, Chad actually was a doctor and had achieved his dream. She was proud of him for that, especially after everything she'd put him through back then. He'd continued on, probably relying on God to see him through the pain Kate inflicted.

How would things have been different if Kate

would have turned to God back then, instead of waiting until she thought she was dying to find her Savior? Maybe then she wouldn't have been so stupid…or so hateful. So self-absorbed. So spiteful.

The list went on and on.

She'd wanted to talk about all of those things today with Chad, to apologize, to explain how she'd changed, to beg for forgiveness.

But he was gone.

Kate leaned her head back and let it rest against the wall. She'd been ready to confess her offenses, ready to learn whether she would receive forgiveness, ready to begin her life again…hopefully with some form of a relationship with the little girl she'd left behind.

She'd have to wait to talk to Chad, but she simply couldn't wait that long to talk to someone about these emotions. Pushing up from the bench, she made a decision. She would talk to someone today, and she knew exactly who that someone should be.

Chapter Eight

"Someone's here!" Dee yelled, scurrying away from the pink dollhouse currently claiming dominion in the center of the living-room floor and running toward the knock at the front door. "Maybe it's Miss Kate!"

"Kay-Kay," Emmie said, taking a little longer to stand from her spot near the dollhouse and then toddling behind her sister.

Mitch had noticed Kate's car wasn't at the B and B when he brought the girls home, so he assumed she was running errands and had planned to check again later to see if she'd returned home. He'd looked forward to seeing her again ever since she left the office, and he was beginning to think of that as a good thing. A positive thing.

"Oh, it's not Miss Kate!" Dee said, peering past the curtain in the sidelight. "It's Aunt Hannah and Autumn!" Dee waved at them through the window while Mitch unlocked the door.

"Autumn?" Emmie asked, attempting to move a little quicker as she padded toward them.

Mitch gave them a smile as he opened the door and hoped he didn't look too disappointed that they were on the other side instead of Kate. "Hey, Hannah."

Her brows were lifted, and she didn't waste a second before saying, "It's me, not Miss Kate." Then one corner of her mouth lifted and she added, "You need to tell me more about this lady."

"Yeah, I suppose I do," he said. He'd decided that he might actually ask Kate out to dinner soon, which would undoubtedly qualify as a date, and he wanted to make sure his family— Jana's family—were okay with that before he asked her. He loved Bo, Maura, Matt and Hannah, and he didn't want to do anything to hurt them, but he also suspected they would understand if he were, finally, ready to start dating again.

"We went to the beach," Autumn said, "and we got you some prizes."

"Prizes? Really? What is it?" Dee asked, now focusing on the large orange bag in Hannah's hand.

Autumn reached into the bag. "I'll show you,"

she said, withdrawing a mesh green bag containing a ball with two Velcro paddles. "This is for you to throw and catch the ball. Daddy and I played it on the beach, and GiGi and I did, too."

Mitch imagined the group on the beach, all of them laughing and playing and having fun, with Maura, aka GiGi, joining in the fun. Maura was one of those grandmothers who didn't merely smile and wave to her grandkids; she got down on the floor and played with them. Or in this case, the sand.

He felt a little regret that he hadn't taken the girls on the trip and given them the chance to play with Autumn on the beach, but then he remembered how much fun they'd had at the park with Kate, and he knew they'd had a good time last week, too. Plus they'd been sick at the beginning of the week, and that would have made for a pretty miserable time at a beach condo.

"And we got you some seashells, too," Autumn said, pulling out another mesh bag filled with shells. "If you hold 'em up by your ear, you can hear the beach! Come here, and I'll show you." She grabbed the bag of shells and turned to take a seat in the center of the porch with Dee and Emmie following.

Hannah shook her head. "She's still got to get the hang of giving presents." Then she said to Autumn, "Hey, don't you think they might have wanted to open their gifts themselves?"

"They like it when I help," Autumn said, picking up a couple of shells and handing one to Dee and another to Emmie. "Okay, now hold it up and listen." She held a shell to her ear to demonstrate.

"Wissen," Emmie said, squinting as she pressed a small pink shell against her ear.

Dee grabbed a larger cream-colored shell and held it against her ear and cheek. "Wow, cool! I think I hear it."

Mitch and Hannah sat on the swing while the girls took turns listening to each shell in the bag to see if they all sounded the same or different. As he suspected, Hannah didn't wait long before asking him about his new employee.

"So, what's Kate's last name? I didn't think to ask when I spoke to her on the phone earlier. Of course, I was a little surprised that you'd hired someone while we were out of town." She cleared her throat. "Not that I think it's bad that you hired someone. You've needed help for so long, and I'm glad you found somebody for the job. It's just odd that she isn't from around here. I mean, not a lot of people just up and move to Claremont, you know?"

"I know." He could have said more, like he still planned to find out exactly what had brought Kate here, but he didn't want to stir her curiosity any more than it already had been. "Her last name is Wydell."

"Wydell." She looked up to the ceiling as she pondered the name, then shook her head. "Nope, I don't believe I've ever known anyone with that name."

"Me, either," he said.

Emmie toddled over to hand him a shell. "Here, Daddy."

"Thanks, sweetie," he said, accepting the tiny gray shell.

"Wissen," she instructed, so Mitch took the shell to his ear.

Sure enough, that whispery sound he associated with seashells was there. "Yes, I hear it."

She clapped, then reached for the shell and went back to join Autumn and Dee.

Hannah and Mitch watched the girls for a moment in silence, and then she said, "So, I guess Kate has been to your house?"

He should've known she wouldn't let Dee's remark go without comment. "Yes," he said. "When she started last week, both of the girls were sick with a virus that's been making its way through the schools. First Emmie, and then Dee. I couldn't take them to day care, but I had a ton of policies to catch up on, so we worked from here."

Her mouth slid to the side. "That...makes sense."

Mitch debated how much to say at this point, because he was only beginning to come to terms with the fact that he wanted to go out with Kate, but he also knew he didn't want to wait long before asking her. So he might as well test the waters with his family. "We took the girls to Hydrangea Park Saturday."

They'd been pushing the swing back and forth slightly, comfortably, as they talked, but Hannah scooted forward so that her flip-flops flattened on the ground and the swing stopped moving. "You and Kate?" she asked.

He nodded.

Apparently Dee had been paying attention to at least a portion of their conversation, because she added, "Miss Kate flew kites with us, and mine went the highest. Daddy had to help Miss Kate and Emmie so theirs didn't blow away," she said with a giggle.

Hannah's brows lifted to disappear beneath her brown bangs.

"Hey, Mommy, can we take the ball and paddles in the yard to play?" Autumn asked.

Hannah turned from Mitch to the girls. "Sure. Just stay on the grass, okay?"

"Okay!"

Autumn and Dee bagged the seashells, while Emmie pushed against the porch floor to stand and then moved toward the swing. "Hold you, Daddy."

Mitch picked her up, kissed her cheek and wondered how long it would take Hannah to ask more about Kate. Didn't take but a moment, about the same amount of time that it took Autumn and Dee to unwrap the paddles and toss the first ball.

"I get the feeling there may be more to Kate than her being your employee," she said. "Am I right?"

Hannah often came across as a protective sister to Mitch, but he didn't really mind. She was the closest thing to a sibling that he'd ever had, and he appreciated the fact that she cared. So he didn't tell her she was being nosy or remind her that it'd been a year and a half since Jana had passed away or that he hadn't even had coffee with another lady since.

Instead, he prepared to tell the truth. "There's something about her—" he started, but Hannah held up a hand.

"Wait," she said. "First I want to say something."

"Okay." Mitch braced himself for the worst, which, in his mind, would be Hannah saying that when he moved on to another relationship they wouldn't be able to maintain their place in his life because it'd be too difficult seeing Mitch with someone other than Jana.

"I just want you to know," she said, "that Matt and I have been praying for this. Maybe not Kate specifically, but we have prayed for God to find someone for you to date again and to eventually give you the courage to love again. Jana wouldn't have wanted you to be alone forever, and neither do we."

Mitch's jaw flexed as he fought to control the emotion her words evoked. They loved him like a son and brother, and they supported him even now, when he considered finally moving on and dating again. "I hope you know how much that means to me, Hannah."

She placed her hand over his on the porch swing and gently squeezed. "You meant everything to my sister, and you'll always be family to us, no matter what."

"Daddy, down," Emmie said, pointing toward the other girls and squirming to get free.

Mitch was thankful for his little lady breaking the tension of his and Hannah's serious conversation. "Sure, you can get down, sweetie. Just let me get you a ball to play with and then I'll help you down the stairs to be with the girls." He got up from the swing and went inside to retrieve Emmie's favorite plastic ball, the one with Strawberry Shortcake on the side, and then returned to find Hannah sitting on the middle porch step. He put Emmie on the grass near Autumn and Dee and gave her the ball. And as soon as he took a seat on the porch step next to Hannah, he saw Kate's car.

Kate looked toward Mitch's house and lifted her hand before she turned in the driveway, and Mitch grinned. "Looks like you may get to meet Kate sooner than you thought."

Hannah straightened on the step. "What? That was her? She's staying at the bed-and-breakfast?"

"For a couple of weeks, while she tries to find a rental house," he said.

"Cool," Hannah said. "I'm looking forward to meeting her. Why don't you see if she wants to come over so I can?"

"Hey, Daddy, look! It's Miss Kate!" Dee yelled, as Kate climbed out of her car. "Miss Kate, come see our new prizes from the beach!"

Mitch's smile grew as he watched Kate start heading their way. "I think Dee's taken care of that for us."

Kate had clearly been shaken up at the community college when she learned Chad was still gone, because she'd honestly thought she would drive to the B and B, walk across the street and divulge the truth about her first marriage and child to Mitch. She wasn't thinking that he'd be involved with taking care of his girls this afternoon. And she also didn't consider the fact that he might have company.

But he was taking care of the girls and he did have company, a pretty brunette sitting on his front porch step beside him, and Kate would simply have to wait until another time to tell her secrets. Disappointment washed through her, but she took a deep breath and hoped it wasn't visible as she crossed the street. Dee had called her over, and there was no way she'd let the girls down by ignoring them.

Another girl, maybe eight or nine years old, called to Dee to watch for the ball. Dee waved to Kate and then turned her attention back to the game the two were playing, while Emmie sat on the grass nearby, laughing as she attempted to kick her own ball.

"Hey, Miss Kate," Dee said. "Did you see how I catched it? Autumn throws me the ball and it sticks right here!" She pointed to the neon green Velcro-covered paddle. "See?"

"Wow, that's really neat, Dee," she said.

"You want to catch with it?" she asked, already starting to undo the strap securing the paddle to her hand.

"No, sweetie, that's okay. You play with Autumn today while she's here, and you can teach me how to play another day."

Kate bit her lower lip. Autumn was Matt and Hannah Graham's little girl, and she hesitated a step before moving closer to the porch. The woman next to Mitch was Hannah, his sister-in-law, and the one person in town who'd actually spent a moment of time with Kate before she left Chad.

"I brought y'all a chicken casserole, some green beans from Daddy's garden and fresh corn." Kate remembered Hannah placing the dishes in their kitchen while Lainey had been crying on Kate's hip. Hannah had been so friendly, so welcoming, and Kate had ushered her out of the house as quickly as possible, because she was already planning how she could leave the clingy husband and screaming baby and get back to Atlanta.

God, please, help me.

"Hey, I'm Hannah. I spoke to you on the phone earlier," Hannah said as Kate neared. "I'm glad Mitch found someone to help him in the office."

Kate smiled, took a step forward and tripped

over the edge of her dress. "Oh," she said, teetering and ending up a little closer to the porch steps than she'd planned. If Hannah were going to recognize her from before, Kate had just made it even easier.

Back when she'd met Hannah the first time, Kate's wardrobe had consisted of sleeveless halter tops, shorts and miniskirts. Now she consistently wore dresses that covered the majority of her thin legs and concealed her pale skin, partly because she was self-conscious about her pallor but even more because she simply wanted to dress modestly. However, today's long dress had nearly landed her in their laps.

Hannah and Mitch both jumped up from their seats in an effort to catch Kate before she fell right into them, but she righted herself and forced an embarrassed smile. "Trust me, I type better than I walk."

Mitch and Hannah both laughed, sat back down and then motioned for Kate to do the same.

"Can you visit with us for a sec?" Hannah asked.

Once she'd seen Mitch had company, Kate hadn't planned to do much more than say hello, but she didn't want to seem rude, so she sat down and thanked God that Hannah didn't appear to have any recollection of meeting her three years ago. "Sure."

"So, where did you live before?" Hannah asked.

"I was in Atlanta. I've spent the majority of my life there, actually," Kate answered, but didn't elaborate.

"And Mitch mentioned you have amazing office-management skills. Where did you work?"

"At a doctor's office in Gwinnett County, northeast of Atlanta," Kate said. She'd actually worked for three different doctors over the past few years, and she'd had affairs with all of them but the last one, for whom she'd started working after the cancer took hold. He was nearing retirement and had a sweet wife whom Kate adored. They were strong Christians and had encouraged her to turn to God instead of giving up. She would forever be grateful to them for that, and she was also grateful for the glowing reference he'd provided to Mitch that allowed her to get the new job.

"Well, I think it's great that Mitch found someone with office-management experience. It's not easy to find anyone in Claremont like that because it's such a small town, and there aren't that many places that even need an office manager." Hannah paused, tilted her head as she studied Kate. "You know, something about you seems so familiar...."

Kate swallowed. "Maybe I have one of those faces, the kind that it seems like you've seen before." She managed a laugh. "Common features."

"I wouldn't say that," Mitch said softly, and Kate found herself turning from Hannah to Mitch, who'd been quietly listening to every word she'd said and had, at some point, scooted a little closer to her on the step.

"Thanks," she whispered, losing herself in the blueness of his eyes and the reddish-blond lashes surrounding them. He was such a unique, interesting man, and he made her feel calm.

Hannah cleared her throat loudly, and Kate blinked, then turned her attention back to the lady still studying her intently but now with a little bit of a smile. "So...what brought you to Claremont?"

Kate noticed Mitch straighten beside her, as though he didn't want Hannah asking this particular question, but Kate didn't mind. She'd give her the same answer she gave him...for now. Later, whenever she got the opportunity to talk to Mitch alone, she'd explain everything. But now she only said, "I wanted to experience small-town living."

Hannah nodded but then squinted at Kate. "You really do seem familiar. Did you do any modeling at some point? We have a store on the square called Consigning Women, where the owner, Maribeth Walton, matches outfits of models and celebrities with the items she has in her store. She'll put the pictures up of the models on the board beside the outfits. Maybe I saw you there?" Her tone was as friendly and inviting as Kate remembered, even if it did feel as if she was getting pleasantly interrogated.

"No, I've never modeled," she said. Then, ready to get away before Hannah put her finger on exactly why she seemed so familiar, Kate stood. "Well, I'm going to get over to the B and B and let y'all continue your visit. It was a pleasure to meet you, Hannah."

"You, too."

Mitch reached for her hand and held it a moment. "I'm glad you came over," he said.

Kate enjoyed the momentary contact, palm to palm, flesh to flesh, the warmth of his hand cloaking hers and making her feel as if everything would somehow be okay. "I'm glad, too," she said.

Still holding her hand, he added, "I'll see you at work in the morning."

"Yes, I'll see you there," she said, then no-

ticed Hannah staring at their joined hands…
and smiling.

"In case anyone's wondering, I'm glad you
came over, too," she said.

Mitch's low laugh caused a sweet tingle along
Kate's spine, and she felt her cheeks blush as she
quickly released his hand. "Thanks, Hannah,"
she said, and then gave each of the girls a hug
before walking back to the B and B.

She was nearly to the opposite sidewalk when
she clearly heard Hannah's next four words to
her brother-in-law.

"I like her, Mitch."

Kate entered the B and B, closed the door
and leaned against it. Then she let her tears of
happiness fall, and she prayed that she wouldn't
shed tears of sadness when Hannah learned who
she was.

Chapter Nine

Kate drove down I-20 from Atlanta toward Claremont thinking about how she couldn't wait for the results of today's checkup to come in. Her oncologist had said if everything came back good again, she could start scheduling her appointments for every six months instead of every three. And then, if she continued having clear reports for another year, her exam would occur annually. The anxiety that she developed for each of these appointments nearly made her as sick as she'd been the days after chemo. This morning she hadn't been able to eat breakfast, and at lunch she hadn't felt any better, so she'd skipped that, too.

She'd been so anxious that she'd hardly said anything to Mitch today beyond answering his questions about work. She'd wanted to ask him more about his visit with Hannah and Autumn, and she'd wondered what he'd thought of Hannah's comment that she liked Kate.

Kate desperately wanted the Claremont community to like her. Maybe it'd be easier to forgive her when they learned who she was if they'd grown to like the new Kate. But Hannah's approval meant even more because she was so close to Mitch.

Kate's stomach growled loudly, obviously ready to make up for that missed breakfast and lunch. She exited the interstate at the next town to pick up something from one of the fast-food restaurants. A cheeseburger sounded really good and should take care of her hunger.

But as she pulled into the Wendy's parking lot, her cell phone rang. Glancing at the display, she saw Mitch's name, so she ignored the drive-through lane and pulled into one of the parking spaces to talk.

"Hello," she answered.

"Hey, how did your appointment go?" he asked.

She still hadn't told him what kind of appointment it was, but she did have a positive feeling about today's checkup, so she answered, "It went good."

"That's great," he said, then he cleared his throat, and the line went silent.

Kate waited, wondering if this was the extent of the conversation. "Well, I guess I'll see you in the morning?" she finally asked, and hoped he'd say that he wanted her to come over and spend time with him and the girls tonight. Even though she'd been gone only this afternoon, she'd missed him, and she'd missed Dee and Emmie, too.

She wondered, if she were able to have a relationship with Lainey, whether this was the type of longing she'd feel toward wanting to see her little girl. Oh, she longed to see her now, but she didn't "know" her like she knew Dee and Emmie. And she wanted to know her. Maybe if her prayers were answered with a yes, she *would* know her daughter very well, very soon.

A couple of cars went through the parking lot to line up at the drive-through while Kate continued waiting for Mitch to say something. Finally, he said, "I'm not all that used to this, but I'm going to give it my best shot here. So bear with me."

He sounded nervous, not like the confident man she'd become so familiar with over the past week, and Kate pressed the phone closer to her ear. "What is it, Mitch?"

"Hannah offered to let the girls stay at their place tonight so they could spend some time with Autumn, since they missed the beach trip. And she thought—or actually, I thought—well, I wondered if you might be hungry and want to have some dinner with me?"

Kate's stomach growled again, loud enough that she thought he might have heard it over the line, and she placed a hand over her mouth because her smile was so broad it hurt. Tears slipped free. Mitch was asking her on a date. A real date. Dinner. Over the past few years, she'd never been the kind of girl a guy took out in public. Harrison Tinsdale was divorced when he and Kate got together, so there was no reason for him to feel the need to keep from taking her out, but once the cancer hit and her weight fell off and she lost her hair, the renowned plastic surgeon opted out of a relationship with a girl who no longer fit his standard for perfection.

"Kate?" Mitch continued, and she realized that now she'd been the one to keep him waiting on the other end.

But she wouldn't keep him waiting any longer. And she wouldn't get that cheeseburger. Dinner with Mitch would be worth the wait. Anything that involved spending time with Mitch would be worth the wait. Tonight, they'd have their first date, and then she'd tell him the truth about Chad and Lainey. For her entire life, she'd done the wrong thing; now she was doing what was right. She could feel it in her soul, and it was a very wonderful, amazingly good feeling. Mitch would forgive her for her past. He would. She'd prayed for it, and she knew her prayers would be answered. Tonight. "Yes, I'd love to go to dinner with you. I should be back to Claremont in about an hour."

"I'll pick you up at six-thirty, then," he said. "And, Kate…"

"Yes?"

"This is my first date in about three years, so I might be a bit rusty."

Kate's heart melted. He was so nervous about starting over again, but little did he know, so was she. "That's okay. It's been that long since I've been on a real date, too, so we'll be rusty together."

Mitch opened the door of the B and B and waited in the foyer, as nervous as a high schooler picking up a girl for their first date and fretting about meeting the parents. But there were no parents to meet.

Then he heard someone bustling down the hall and realized he'd been wrong. She wasn't a parent, but he had no doubt Annette Tingle had already taken on a motherly type role in Kate's world, and the way she looked at him now, her eyes expectant and inquisitive, Mitch prepared for something akin to the high school drilling. *Where are you going? When will you be back? What are you planning to do while you're gone?*

Mrs. Tingle said, "Kate is still getting ready. She'll be down in a moment. Why don't we wait on the porch?"

"Okay," Mitch said, thinking there was probably a reason she ushered him outside and then closed the door instead of allowing him to wait in the foyer.

His suspicions proved true when she lowered her voice and said, "This means a lot to Kate, you asking her to dinner this evening, and I wanted you to know I think it's a good thing, too, for her and for you." Then she glanced back toward the door, still closed, and added in a whisper, "She's been hurt in the past, and she's hurt folks in the past. I don't know the specifics, but I know that that sweet girl has been through a lot and that she's trying to find her way again. And I honestly think God sent her here to do that."

"She's talked to you?" he asked, curious as to whether Annette knew about the child or about whatever else had happened in Kate's past.

"Like I said, nothing specific, only to say that

she's not sure she deserves forgiveness for what she's done. Breaks my heart, let me tell you."

Mitch hurt for Kate, feeling so terrible about letting her baby go. He wanted to help her find the forgiveness she needed and learn to live again. Maybe even learn to love again, if that was where this relationship headed. Because Mitch had started to think that it might be possible for him again…with Kate. Tonight was merely the first step in seeing if that possibility could become probability and then ultimately reality.

The door opened, Kate stepped out and Mitch was momentarily speechless. She wore a long royal-blue dress, more classy than any of the dresses she'd worn to the office or to church. Tiny spaghetti straps held it in place on her slender shoulders, and a layer of lace, the same hue as the dress, covered the fabric and hung a little lower than the hem, drawing attention to her gold sandals and pink-painted toes. Her dark curls were pinned up on the sides with gold barrettes, and that gold locket that she often wore dangled beneath her neck. She looked so feminine, so beautiful.

And Mitch had to tell her. "You look…stunning."

The spot between her neck and that locket

blushed pink. "Thank you," she said, touching that very place as if she could feel her heated skin. "I'm sorry you had to wait, but I had a hard time picking what to wear."

"I like what you chose," he said. "That color matches your eyes, makes them even bluer, I think."

Mrs. Tingle nodded her agreement. "I think so, too." Then she smiled at Mitch, gave Kate a hug and kissed her cheek. "Y'all have a good time," she said, still smiling as she went back into the house.

And then the two of them stood on the porch, alone and anxious. Mitch cleared his throat. "So, you ready to go?"

She nodded. "I am."

Mitch stepped toward her and thought about putting his arm around her as he walked her to the car, but it didn't seem the right thing to do, at least not yet. So he walked beside her, holding out a hand to help her as they went down the porch steps, since she used one hand to hold up the lacy hem of her dress. It felt good to help her, felt right to hold her hand, so when they reached the bottom of the steps, Mitch didn't let go. And she didn't pull away.

A tiny measure of success trickled through him, and he found himself feeling a bit of ease at this first-date thing. He opened the passenger door and watched her gather the blue fabric to puddle around her legs as she climbed in. She was so graceful. So...*fragile,* his mind whispered. Fragile. Why did he get that impression? Maybe because of Mrs. Tingle's comments that Kate had been hurt and that she also felt the pain of having hurt others. Mitch assumed that had something to do with when she gave up her child. He wanted to help her through those pains, but he'd have to wait until she trusted him enough to open up. Maybe she would start tonight.

He circled the car and got in the driver's seat to find Kate holding up a tiny pink Hello Kitty bag.

"I'm thinking this isn't for me?" she asked.

He laughed. "Hannah called to say the girls forgot their toothbrushes, so I thought we'd drop them off at their place before we go to the restaurant, if that's okay."

She placed the bag in her lap. "Of course it's fine."

Mitch backed the car up and started the short drive to Matt and Hannah's home. They lived in a subdivision on the other side of Hydrangea Park, and when they neared the park, Mitch noticed the Little League fields were packed.

"Looks like a few T-ball games going on to-night," he said, slowing the car to watch a tiny batter hit the ball off the tee and take off running toward first base while the crowd of parents cheered. The little girl's blond ponytail bounced against her back as she ran. She stumbled and fell onto the base but then jumped up and started clapping. Mitch chuckled. "They get to play when they're four. Dee just missed the cutoff this year, but she's already said she wants to play next year. I'm looking forward to that."

"Oh, my, I didn't realize girls played T-ball, too. That's a girls' team?" She peered out the window to see the next batter, a little boy who had turned away from the tee completely to wave at his family in the stands. "No, that's a little boy," she said, answering her question before Mitch had the chance.

"Right. At that age, it's all about having fun and bringing the community together. They don't even keep score, and they don't worry about separating the boys from the girls." He continued past the fields. "In a small town, athletics are a pretty big deal because it gives folks something to do, and it usually keeps the teenagers out of trouble, or that's what my folks always said. Seemed to work for me, though I wasn't perfect or anything," he clarified.

"I wasn't perfect, either," she whispered, her face still turned away from Mitch as she peered toward the fields until they disappeared. He was fairly certain she hadn't intended for him to hear the remark, so he didn't ask any questions. Yet. He wanted her to tell him about her past without him feeling as though he were dissecting it. So he went with a safer point of discussion.

"I'm guessing girls didn't play T-ball where you grew up in Atlanta?" he asked, glancing at her and seeing that she appeared to be pondering the answer.

"You know, I'm really not sure. I had two stepsisters, but they were much older and didn't care for sports at all. And my stepmom and father didn't sign me up for it, if T-ball were an option for me. As a matter of fact, I don't think I've ever seen a T-ball game."

"Well, we'll have to change that," he said. "If not this year, then definitely next year when Dee plays." He liked the idea of Kate being with him next year and cheering Dee on when she played. He liked it a lot, in fact.

Still trying to learn a bit about her childhood and then hopefully her adulthood, he continued, "So, what types of activities did you do as a kid? Soccer? Swim team? Karate? Or maybe you were more of an art and piano lessons kind of girl? I've been looking into all of the options for Dee and Emmie, and it's almost overwhelming. I don't want to pick too many and burn them out, but I also want to help them find their talents and interests."

Kate turned to look at him, and she gave him a soft smile. "You really are an amazing daddy, you know that?"

"I'm trying," he said with a grin. "So, what did you like? Maybe that'll help me know which direction to start when I begin signing Dee and Emmie up for activities."

She shook her head. "To tell the truth, I don't know what I would have liked at that age. Apart from things at the day care and then school, I didn't do any activities that I can recall."

"Nothing?" he asked, shocked.

"My father and stepmom worked late hours at their jobs, so they didn't have time to take me to practices. I was typically the last one picked up from the after-school program. We'd eat dinner, then I'd do homework and get ready for bed, and then the next day, it'd start again," she said. "I hope my little girl gets to do lots of activities, though."

"I hope so, too," he said, wishing he didn't hear so much sadness and regret in her words. Mitch knew her thoughts revolved daily around that little girl she didn't know. Wondering about her, longing for her, missing her. He now suspected that Kate's own childhood may have played a part in her deciding to give up her daughter. From just the brief conversations they'd had, he hadn't detected a lot of love in the family, nor an abundance of time for familial bonding.

Mitch loved his time in the afternoons with Dee and Emmie, listening to them chatter about their day and about their friends, playing games with them and growing closer to them. From the sound of things, Kate must have spent the majority of her afternoons waiting for her folks to pick her up. There was no affection in her voice when she mentioned them, no hint of happy childhood reminiscence. Surely there was something she enjoyed and was able to participate in growing up. "How about once you got older, in middle school or high school?" he asked. "What did you like then?"

Luckily, he glanced at her at just the right moment to see her face transform and light up with excitement. "I liked to run. Or rather, I *loved* to run."

Have mercy, she was so pretty when she smiled. Mitch made a mental note to do whatever it took to make certain she smiled often. All the time. "Did you run track for your school?"

She nodded. "Junior high and high school. I'd thought I might get a scholarship and get to run in college, but I wasn't that good. I did enjoy it, though. There's so much freedom when you run, don't you think?"

He thought about her thin frame and should have realized that she might be a long-distance runner. That was the kind of build they had, thin, lean, not necessarily built for speed as much as endurance. "What did you run? The 1600-meter? Cross-country?"

"Oh, no, I never was that good at long distances. Nothing farther than a hundred meters for me. The 4x100-meter relay, the 100-meter dash, 200-meter dash, 400-meter dash. Pretty much, if it was a 'dash,' it was my race."

Mitch was floored. Those were the high-speed runs, the ones typically reserved for the strongest and fastest athletes. Kate didn't look like that kind of runner, but undoubtedly he was being reminded that looks could be deceiving. "You were a sprinter?" He meant to mask his shock but failed, because she laughed.

"Don't sound so surprised. I was actually fairly quick once upon a time."

"Oh, hey, I didn't mean it like that. It's just that you don't look like a sprinter."

"I used to," she said but didn't offer any other explanation.

"So, what leg were you on the 4x100 relay?" he asked, as he pulled into Matt and Hannah's driveway, where the girls were all out playing in the front yard.

"Fourth," she said.

Mitch glanced to see she was smiling smugly. "You were the last leg? Fastest on the team, weren't you?"

"I'm sure there have been faster times since, but back then I was."

Mitch processed what she didn't say. "You held the school record?"

"For a while," she said, then waved at Dee and Emmie through the front car window. "Looks like they're having fun."

Mitch turned off the car and waited while the girls stopped playing and started toward the car. "There's a lot about you that I still need to learn," he said.

A look passed over her face, something Mitch couldn't read, and she answered, "I plan on telling you everything, though. Just give me time." She grabbed the Hello Kitty bag and stepped out of the car to meet the girls, both running to her side instead of Mitch's.

Mitch smiled, happy Dee and Emmie liked Kate so much, and also happy to give her the time she needed to tell him about her past. He was eager to discover everything he could about the woman who had apparently been an impressive sprinter not that long ago. What other surprises would he learn as he got to know the beauty currently accepting hugs from his girls and slowly but surely intriguing his heart?

Matt, Hannah and Autumn neared Mitch's side of the car, while Dee and Emmie gave Kate another hug and then came around to give their daddy a hug, too.

"Love you, Daddy," Dee said, holding him tight.

"Wuv Daddy," Emmie said when he hugged her.

Dee handed the Hello Kitty bag to Hannah. "Here, Aunt Hannah. Will you hold this so we can play a little more on the swing set? It's almost dark, so we gotta hurry."

"Yes, I'll hold it," Hannah said, accepting the tiny bag and then grinning as the girls ran off.

Matt smiled toward Kate, and Mitch realized he hadn't introduced them. "Oh, Matt, this is

Kate. Kate, this is Matt Graham, my brother-in-law."

"Nice to meet you," Kate said.

"You, too," Matt responded, while Hannah squinted toward Kate.

"I think it *must* be one of those model pictures at Consigning Women that I'm thinking of when I see you."

"Do they have any photos of Snow White?" Mitch asked jokingly. "Dee seems to think she's the spitting image."

"I can see that," Hannah said. "You really could be a model, you know."

"Oh, no, I don't think so," Kate said, "but thank you."

"She could be a runner, though," Mitch said, grinning. "A sprinter, in fact."

"A sprinter?" Matt asked.

Kate shrugged. "I ran track in high school. That's it."

"And she held the school record," Mitch added, enjoying watching her blush.

"Okay now, that's enough about me," Kate said. "It was nice seeing you again, Hannah. Pleasure to meet you, Matt," she said and then got in the car.

"I think that's my signal that I've embarrassed her and that it's time to go eat," Mitch said.

Matt winked at him. "Good to see ya happy."

Mitch nodded, realizing that he did feel genuinely happy. "Thanks."

He got in the car and they waved goodbye as they turned around and then started out of the driveway.

"For someone who's wanting me to share everything, you sure are finding it mighty fun to embarrass me," she said, but her tone was more flirtatious than reprimanding. Then she pinched his biceps. "See if I tell you anything again."

He winked at her. "You will."

"How can you be so sure?" she asked, still flirting and still making Mitch grin.

"Because I want to know…and I'll ask nicely," he said.

She laughed. "You aren't lacking for confidence, are you?"

"Truthfully, when I picked you up tonight, I felt like a fish out of water. Nervous, I'd say. But yeah, my confidence is making a reappearance."

"Why's that?" she asked.

"Because I can tell you're starting to have a good time. Aren't ya?"

"You know, I really am." Her stomach growled so loudly that if Mitch hadn't known it was Kate he'd have said that could've only come from a very large, famished man.

"Hungry?" he asked.

She laughed almost as loudly as her stomach had growled. "I haven't eaten today. I was going to get a cheeseburger when you called me on the way home, and then I decided to hold out so I'd be good and hungry for dinner."

"Based on that sound, I'd say you're there."

She laughed again. "And I'd say you're right."

"We're going to a steak house in Stockville," he said. "How does a salad, filet mignon, baked potato and then blackberry cobbler with ice cream sound?"

Her stomach answered with another growl, and she giggled. "Talk about embarrassing."

"I think it's adorable," he said honestly.

"I don't know if I can hold all of that food," she said, "but I'm pretty sure I'd like to make an effort."

Kate walked out of the restaurant with Mitch after indulging in one of the most delicious meals she'd ever eaten. "That was amazing," she said as they reached his car and he opened her door.

"I know," he agreed while she climbed in. "I'd have never thought someone as tiny as you could eat so much. Amazing." Then he closed

her door amid her gasps and rounded the car…
but not before Kate clicked the lock button.

Mitch tried the handle and then realized what
she'd done and started laughing. He tapped on
the window. "Hey, let me in."

"Those are *so* not the right words," she said,
flipping the visor down and checking her lipstick in the lit mirror while she ignored the guy
locked out of the car.

Mitch loved it. He tapped on the window
again. "Please, Kate. Forgive me, and let me in."

She snapped the visor closed and leaned
across the seat, blue eyes capturing the street
light and glittering mischievously. "What was
that first word again?" she asked.

He smirked. *"Please."*

She nodded. "Yep, that's the right one." Then
she clicked the unlock button and giggled when
he got in.

"But you did eat more than me," he said,
cranking the engine while she punched him.

"Hey, I hadn't eaten all day. I told you that,
and I was hungry."

"Obviously." Then he laughed again, and she
joined in, unable to remember the last time she'd
laughed so much. The entire night had been
filled with good conversation, great food and an
abundance of laughter. It was an amazing date,

and Kate didn't want to ruin it by bringing up the mistakes of her past. Yes, she'd planned to talk to Mitch tonight about Chad and Lainey, but the opportunity simply wasn't there. She'd tell him, but she wouldn't mar this perfect night with something sad. Besides, from the way the date had gone, she suspected they'd have another soon. And that was when she'd tell him. Not tonight, when her skin tingled with excitement, with happiness and with hope.

Hope. That was what she felt more than anything else. And *that* was what had been missing in her life most of all.

By the time he pulled into the driveway at the B and B, they'd laughed and joked the entire drive home.

"Looks like Mrs. Tingle left the light on for you," he said, pointing to the bright beam illuminating the entire porch. "Kind of adds to the whole first-date feeling, doesn't it?"

Kate grinned. "She has become something of a mom to me since I've been here, and I can't deny I like it."

"I like having you across the street, too," he said. "Gotta admit, I'm going to be a bit bummed when you move to the rental house. And the girls will, too. So you're going to have to come visit often, or we'll come to you."

"Promise?" she asked.

"Definitely."

"I haven't found the time to even look for a rental yet. I actually told Mrs. Tingle today that I'll probably go ahead and stay at the B and B at least a couple more weeks and maybe even all of June."

"I'm rather happy you haven't found a place yet," he said, opening his door and climbing out.

Kate watched him cross in front of the car, his tall frame blocking the light from the porch as he moved purposefully to open her door. She was drawn to that confidence that exuded from his very soul. Being around Mitch made her feel safe, happy, hopeful.

She climbed out, very much aware of his presence as she stepped by him and they walked toward the porch. Midway up the sidewalk, his hand found hers, palms touching gently as their fingers intertwined. And just like that, the laughter that had been on the edge of Kate's tongue all night and had released so freely was exchanged for something else entirely. She wanted to keep feeling his hand in hers and wanted to feel his arms around her once more, like they'd been last Saturday at the park.

When they reached the door, she turned to

thank him. "I had an incredible time tonight," she said.

"No problems with me being rusty? I did okay?"

"Very okay," she said. "How about me? Any problems with me being rusty on the dating?"

He grinned. "Not at all. But, I've got to tell you, there's another area I might be rusty at, too, and you'll just have to give me an honest answer about it." He stepped closer, and Kate watched his gaze fall from her eyes to her lips.

She swallowed. "Okay."

Then he placed his fingertips at her temples, slowly edged them down her cheeks and jaw, before gently tilting her chin and easing his lips to hers.

The brush of his mouth was feather-soft, and Kate found herself pressing her lips against his kiss, enjoying the warmth of him, the tenderness of his touch, an almost reverent sensation, as though she were something precious. Something treasured.

As gently as he started, he eased their lips apart to end the kiss, and Kate immediately wanted more. Mitch, she suspected, could see that in her eyes, because he touched a finger to her trembling lower lip and then gave her another soft kiss.

"So, am I rusty?" he asked, his confident smile saying he knew her answer, as if the soft moan she'd emitted somewhere in the middle of that kiss didn't give her away.

"You are anything but rusty," she said honestly. Then, because she now wondered if he'd felt anything near what she did, she asked, "How about me?"

"You're..." he said, pausing as he appeared to contemplate the right word. "You're captivating, intriguing and mesmerizing."

"Wow," she whispered.

"I was thinking the same thing." He reached past her and opened the door. "Good night, Kate. I'll see you in the morning."

She wanted another kiss, but she wouldn't be greedy. "See you in the morning." Then she entered the B and B, made her way to her room and fell onto the bed smiling.

Mitch backed his car out and drove it the short distance to park in his own driveway across the street. He glanced at the top bay window of the B and B, where Kate would soon be sleeping. He'd told her the truth. He found her captivating, intriguing and mesmerizing. And he wanted to continue learning more about the fascinating lady who'd seemed to have been sent to his world directly from God. She was everything he'd prayed for, even if he hadn't realized that he was ready for anything beyond a capable office manager.

He *was* ready to move on to a relationship again. He could feel it so thoroughly, he had no doubt. And even his in-laws supported this. Hannah had told him so last night, and then Matt also seemed thrilled that Mitch was dating again. He knew Bo and Maura would feel the same. That meant so much to Mitch, to have their support.

His cell phone rang as he entered the house. He glanced at the display and saw Hannah's name.

Mitch answered. "I was just thinking about y'all. Oh, hey, is everything okay with the girls? Is something wrong?" Concern quickly filled him as he remembered Matt and Hannah were keeping Dee and Emmie.

"They're fine," Hannah said. "I should've thought you'd wonder if something was wrong, and I asked Matt if I should wait until morning before calling, but then I couldn't sleep for thinking about it, and I just had to call and tell you. Mitch, I feel awful, but I think I have to say something. I mean, I'd want to know, and you need to know. And I'm still just so shocked by it all."

Hannah rattled off the words so quickly that Mitch had a hard time keeping up, and from what he could tell, nothing made sense. "Hannah, is something wrong?"

"Yes, something is very wrong. Tonight, when I saw her dressed up, it sparked the memory a little clearer. Because that time I met her, even though she wore a halter and shorts, her makeup was done just so and her hair fixed beautifully, like she were going out on a date. Her face is different now, thinner or something. It makes her eyes appear a little bigger. Her hair is the biggest difference, though. It was long and blond. And she was very tan. There's just so many differences, but the more I thought about it and then also the fact that she moved to Claremont from Atlanta, the more I knew I was right."

Again, Mitch was clueless, but he could tell this had something to do with Kate. "Hannah, what are you trying to say?"

"Kate. She looked so familiar because I did meet her before." She paused and then said, "It was when she was married to Chad Martin."

Chapter Ten

Since Hannah was taking the girls to the day care this morning, Mitch came in to the office extra early to give himself time to prepare for the arrival of his office manager. But how did you prepare for someone who had so thoroughly lied to you since the moment she'd stepped foot through your door?

The entire town knew the story about Chad's first wife. She'd essentially destroyed him, or at least attempted to, by having him give up his dream of being a medical doctor, move back to Claremont in an effort to keep her happy and then leaving him with a baby to raise…and no way to understand why she'd treated him so badly.

Mitch had been up most of the night trying to reconcile Kate Martin with Kate Wydell, the woman who, only yesterday, he'd thought he was falling in love with.

Obviously Chad wasn't the only male she was doing a number on.

Mitch pressed his pen against the desk as he remembered every horrible detail he'd known about the woman back then. She'd met Chad in Atlanta when he was still recovering from his first love, Jessica, leaving Claremont without telling him goodbye. Chad had no idea that Jess had been pregnant, or that she'd left because she didn't want him to give up his scholarship to marry her. So the guy was already down and vulnerable, and then he met Kate.

Chad had been smitten from the get-go by the gorgeous blonde with a zest for life and a penchant for the adventurous.

Mitch had met his friend's ex-wife once, but he didn't see Kate as the girl from his memory. Her dark curls were different from the long, silky blond hair he remembered, and Mitch hadn't seen any hint of a woman who lived for hiking, white-water rafting and snow skiing. Those were characteristics of the girl Chad had married back then. Kate seemed more like the sit-around-and-watch-a-T-ball-game type girl. Happy to merely play with Dee and Emmie in the front yard.

Chad had said he couldn't keep up with her craving for action when he had to study so much for med school, but he also said he didn't realize how badly she wanted him to become a doctor until he dropped out to save their marriage.

And then there was what she did to Chad regarding Lainey. Which was, basically, one of the most mean-spirited actions Mitch had ever heard of.

The pen bent beneath the weight of Mitch's fingers and snapped in two, spraying ink all over the desk, his papers and even on his dress shirt.

He picked up the pieces and flung them across the room.

And that was when his employee walked in.

Kate opened the office door at the precise moment that a plastic hunk of pen landed a few feet in front of her, spraying ink in its wake. She glanced toward Mitch's desk and saw that the remainder of the pen had apparently headed the opposite direction and the majority of the ink had landed all over and around her boss.

She'd woken in a happy mood, the memory of Mitch's kiss keeping a smile on her face, so now, seeing this scene made her giggle. "Oh, my, bless your heart," she said, closing the door behind her and tossing her purse on the top of her desk. "Let me go get some napkins or a towel out of the back and help you get cleaned up." She started quickly maneuvering through the front office, but then noticed his eyes zeroed in on her, his mouth flattened and tense.

Especially after their date last night, when the majority of the time they'd been laughing, she didn't understand why he was this upset over a broken pen. "Mitch, is something wrong? Is it the girls? Are Dee and Emmie sick again? Because I can run things here, and you can go take care of them. Or we could work from your house again, if you'd rather."

"The only thing wrong with the girls, the way I see it," he said, his words clipped and short, as though he were forcing them through a clenched jaw, "is that they've gotten so attached to you."

Kate stopped, stood stone-still and braced for the worst. "What?"

"That's what happened before, isn't it? People would get attached to you, fall for you, and then once you didn't need them anymore, you left them." He shook his head. "You nearly destroyed Chad, broke his faith and shattered his confidence. Do you know how hard it was for him after you left?"

Kate's head pounded at the rapid change of

events. He knew…and she had missed the opportunity to tell him herself. "I am so sorry for everything I did and for everyone I hurt," she said. Last night she thought she might be falling in love with Mitch, and she'd prayed he might be feeling the same thing. And now he looked at her as though she disgusted him, as though he hated the fact that she'd ever entered his life.

And maybe he did.

"I won't let you hurt my girls that way, get them attached and then leave them behind. They don't deserve that." He paused. "No one deserves that."

"I need to explain," she said, struggling to pick the right words with her blood pumping so fast it burned within her veins. "I was going to tell you—"

"When?" he yelled. "Exactly when were you going to tell me, Kate? After I completely lost my heart to you? After I fell in love with you? After my girls started seeing you as a part of their lives? When?"

She backed up until her hip hit the desk and then she got a bearing on her emotions. He'd just spouted everything she had hoped would happen. That he would lose his heart to her, that he would fall in love with her and that she'd become a part of Dee's and Emmie's lives for good. And Lainey's. *Help me out, Lord. Please, let me say the right thing. I've hurt him. Help me fix that, Lord. I think I may be falling in love with him, and I don't want to ruin this relationship before it even gets started.*

"I was going to tell you last night," she said.

One brow lifted, and his mouth slid into a sneer. "I don't recall you mentioning needing to tell me something."

"That's because I couldn't."

"Couldn't, or wouldn't?" he asked. "Do you realize I haven't been on a date with anyone but my late wife?"

"I know, and that's part of why I didn't want to ruin our perfect night by bringing up my past. I knew I had to tell you, and I wanted to tell you. I still do! But last night was one of the most beautiful nights of my life, and I knew you hadn't been out with anyone else since Jana passed away."

"Ever," he said. The word snapped out as though he wished it could inflict physical pain.

But Kate didn't know what he meant. "Ever? What?"

"I've never been on a date with anyone but Jana. Asking you out was huge for me. It meant more than merely a date. It meant…that I felt something toward you and that I thought there might be a possibility in commitment. That's the way I am, Kate. That's the way I've always been. When I do something, I don't do it halfway, and I certainly don't do it for my own selfish means. I asked you out because I thought you might be special, that God might have sent you here purposely...for me."

His honesty was more painful than any lies Kate had ever been told, because she could see the truth of his words in his eyes, and she could see the pain that she'd inflicted by holding back her truth.

"Let me tell you everything, Mitch, please. Because I want the same things that you do, and I don't want last night to be my only time spent with you. Please, let me tell you about everything back then."

He wadded up the top sheets of ink-covered papers on his desk and tossed them in the trash. Then those blue eyes that Kate had always seen so much compassion in looked up at her, but she saw only revulsion now. "No, Kate, why don't I tell you about everything back then. You met Chad in Atlanta after he'd been abandoned by the love of his life. He was alone in a new city and he was heartbroken. You were, according to Chad, one of the most beautiful girls he'd ever seen, and you had a zest for life that enamored him, because he had basically been ready to give up on life. You had a great big dream of marrying a doctor, and you set your sights on Chad because he was in med school and he was also vulnerable and easy to manipulate." He waited a beat. "Let me know if anything I say isn't true."

Kate gripped the desk to keep her hands from shaking. "It's all true," she whispered, "and it's what I was going to tell you last night."

He gave her a single nod that said he didn't believe her. "Then he asked you to marry him, and you said yes. It all happened so quickly, the intense dating and then running off to Vegas, that all of us in Claremont merely knew our buddy had fallen head over heels and gotten married. I was actually happy for him."

"I'm sorry for what I put him through," she said. "I am, Mitch."

"Is it true that your friend called him when you were trying to abort Lainey?" Mitch asked, his voice no longer angry but converting to something that sounded pained. "Is it, Kate?"

"I did go to the clinic, but I didn't do it," she said. And then, before Mitch could tell her what she was certain he already knew, she added, "But Chad came to the clinic and stopped me."

"And then you were miserable," he said. "You

didn't like being pregnant, and you didn't like being married to Chad while he spent all of his time working on his med degree. You wanted to marry a doctor, but you weren't willing to go through the intern years so that he could be... good enough for you."

"I've changed, Mitch. I have, and that's why I came to Claremont. I want to show Chad that I've changed and I want to have a relationship with Lainey. I want to be her mother."

He moved his hand to his forehead and then pinched the bridge of his nose. "You see, that's the thing that I remember the most, the part where you not only left Chad to raise Lainey, but you twisted the knife. You told him that you'd never wanted to have her anyway and that if he wanted her he could have her...but that she wasn't biologically his."

Kate's sob tore through the room, the pain of that moment, of recalling the horrified look on Chad's face when she'd told him he wasn't Lainey's father and then slammed the door without ever looking back. "Chad loved her, whether she was his or not. I knew he did. I knew he would be better to her, be better for her, than I would be."

"But that isn't why you left her with Chad, Kate. You weren't doing what was best for

Lainey. You were doing what was best for you. Right?" He slammed his palm on the desk and repeated louder, "Right?"

"I'm sorry. Sorry for what I did back then and sorry for what I've done to you now. I never meant to hurt you, and I would never ever hurt Dee and Emmie, I promise. Please believe me, Mitch."

This time, he tilted his head back and looked at the ceiling, and Kate was almost certain she saw a tear leak from his eye and streak down his cheek. "How would I know whether to ever believe you, Kate, when you nearly killed him with your deceit? Chad believed you back then. What if you're doing it again? What if you're here playing me so that I'll convince him to let you see Lainey?" His words were spoken toward the ceiling, but then he lowered his chin and looked at Kate. "You're obviously very good at manipulating, and you're definitely a pro at keeping secrets. Just look at the secrets you've kept from me ever since the day you got here."

"I *was* going to tell you, and I did tell you that I gave up my little girl."

"I thought you meant by adoption, not that you walked out on a husband and daughter because you were chasing doctors in Atlanta."

His words pierced her heart, but Kate couldn't

deny that they were true. "I was going to explain it all, in detail."

"When?"

"Before Chad got back from vacation," she said honestly. But she had no idea whether he'd believe her now. Or ever.

He shook his head. "I don't have anything else to say to you, Kate. I don't understand. I've been trying all night to wrap my mind around why. Why are you back in Claremont? Why did you apply for a job at my office knowing Chad and I are friends? And why didn't you tell me the truth about who you were when you had to see I was falling for you?"

He *was* falling for her. But he wasn't now. And from the look on his face, he never wanted to see her again. Which, Kate supposed, served her right for the pain she'd caused in the past. She felt the dampness on her dress and realized that her tears had been steadily falling throughout their heated conversation, but she didn't wipe them away now. They'd serve as a reminder of what she'd done and a reminder of what she'd lost. She picked up her purse, turned and walked out of the office and out of Mitch's life.

Chapter Eleven

Kate rushed up the steps of the B and B and hurried to her room, thankful that none of the other guests or the Tingles had been in her path. She could barely breathe, much less attempt to speak. She rushed to the closet and, heaving through her tears, grabbed her suitcase. Coming back to Claremont had been a mistake. Everything Mitch said, everything he felt, would only be magnified by the man she'd hurt most of all. Chad wouldn't let her have a place in Lainey's world. Why would he?

Her sucking sobs filled the air as she gathered her clothes and were so loud that she must not have heard the knock on her bedroom door, because she jumped when Mrs. Tingle entered.

"I'm sorry I startled you," she said.

Kate dropped the shoes in her arms onto the bed and wiped at her cheeks. "It's okay."

The sweet lady nodded, moved toward the bed, scooted the suitcase over and sat down. "You were crying so hard that I could hear you downstairs."

Kate swiped again at her wet face, looked at the back of her palm and saw an abundance of mascara mess. "I must look awful."

"No, you look like a girl with a broken heart. Mitch, I guess? And are you going somewhere?" She placed a hand on the edge of the suitcase. "Because I thought you'd actually decided to stay here a little longer. You said you hadn't found a rental house yet."

Kate knew the lady was smarter than that. She could tell Kate wasn't merely packing to move to a different location in town; she was packing to leave, to run away from the pain she felt…and the pain she'd caused. "I'm leaving Claremont, Mrs. Tingle. I shouldn't have come back, and I don't want to hurt anyone else."

Mrs. Tingle frowned. "You shouldn't have come *back*?"

Kate had started gathering her makeup and putting it in her cosmetics case, but she stopped, took a deep breath and decided to tell the kind lady the truth. "Wydell is my maiden name, and my legal name now, but before—three years ago—my last name was Martin. Kate Martin."

It took only a couple of seconds for Mrs. Tingle's eyes to widen, her hand to move over her mouth, and then she mumbled against her fingers, "Oh, my. Oh, Kate."

"I came back because I wanted to do the right thing, and I really wanted to have a relationship—some kind of relationship—with my little girl."

Her hand still over her mouth, Mrs. Tingle continued, "Lainey. Lainey is your little girl."

Kate nodded. "And I haven't seen her in three and a half years. She was only six months old when I left." She glanced down to the locket around her neck, ran her thumbnail beneath the edge of the gold and opened it. The only picture she had of Lainey, the one Chad had given her when she was still in the hospital after giving birth, stared back. A newborn baby with a sprinkle of fine blond curls and bright blue eyes.

Tears leaked from Mrs. Tingle's eyes. "Everyone loves Lainey," she whispered, leaning over to peek at the photo in the locket. "Oh, dear. Chad and Jessica."

Jessica. Chad's first love. Mother of his son and the only mother Lainey had ever known. Kate was actually grateful that Lainey had someone who had adopted her and loved her as though she were her own. Basically, that was what Chad had done, after he'd learned Lainey wasn't his child.

"I know that Jessica is her mother now. And I wasn't going to try to take that from her. I just wanted—hoped—that they might find it in their hearts to let me have some place in her life, too." Kate's temples throbbed, and she sat on the bed because she felt as though she might pass out if she continued standing. "But Mitch was so angry, and if he was that mad at me, then I can only imagine how mad Chad will be."

Mrs. Tingle reached out and placed her hand over Kate's, her fingers damp from wiping away tears. "It's just because this is, well, such a shock, dear. Having you come back now and after everything that happened back then. You need to give them time, time to realize and understand that you've changed and time to consider how they can let you be a part of Lainey's world." She pointed to the suitcase. "Leaving isn't going to solve anything."

"But what if they can't forgive me? What if they never want me to see Lainey again?" She sniffed. "What if Mitch never wants to see me again?"

Mrs. Tingle's lower lip rolled in as she thought about Kate's questions, and then she nodded. "You know, my mama always told me that if you wanted to try and figure out the reason a person was acting a certain way, you needed to put yourself in their shoes. Think about this from Mitch's perspective. Everything he's heard about you has been negative. He knows you as a person who deceived one of his friends, and the type of loyalty a man like Mitch has keeps him from wanting to do anything that would allow one of his friends to get hurt. Perhaps he's thinking that he will be hurting Chad if he befriends you, and even more if he had a relationship with you."

Kate shook her head. "I don't think that's it, Mrs. Tingle, or not entirely. He was angry because he thinks I'm going to do the same thing to him, and to his girls." She squeezed Annette's hand and said, "I wouldn't. I'd never hurt him or Dee or Emmie. But he doesn't believe me, and I don't think he ever will."

"You see, that's the thing about Mitch. And Chad, too, for that matter. They're good, honest men, and they both love their Lord. And you can't truly love your Lord without understanding a thing or two about forgiveness."

Kate thought about that, but then she remembered Mitch's words.

"How would I know whether to ever believe you, Kate, when you nearly killed him with your

deceit? Chad believed you back then. What if you're doing it again? What if you're here playing me so that I'll convince him to let you see Lainey? You're obviously very good at manipulating, and you're definitely a pro at keeping secrets. Just look at the secrets you've kept from me ever since the day you got here."

"Even if they did forgive me for what I did in the past, I can't see either of them forgetting. Or trusting me again."

"You need to give them time, honey," Mrs. Tingle said. "They're still coming to terms with learning who you are."

"Chad still doesn't know," Kate whispered. "I haven't had a chance to tell him, because he's been on vacation ever since I got here. I could try to call him, but it didn't seem like the thing to tell someone over the phone. But I can't see him acting any differently than Mitch did. He may hate me even more for what I did to him back then."

"Like I said, you need to give them time." She lifted the small stack of nightshirts out of Kate's suitcase, walked over to the dresser and put them in the top drawer. "Running away isn't the answer to dealing with problems. If you never face them, they will come find you." She closed the drawer and asked, "Did Mitch fire you?"

"He didn't use those words," Kate said.

"What words did he use?"

Kate swallowed, remembering all of the things Mitch had said and shedding a few more tears at the hurt—and anger—in his tone. "He didn't say anything about my work, exactly, but he definitely didn't want me around, so I left."

"So you're taking a day off."

Kate couldn't help it; she smiled for the first time since she'd walked in the office this morning. "I don't think Mitch would see it that way. I'm pretty sure he isn't expecting to see me there again. Ever."

"We'll see. In the meantime," Mrs. Tingle said, steadily unpacking Kate's bag as she spoke, "you should take advantage of the day off to pray and ask God what He thinks you should do, then relax awhile. There are some really good romance novels in the top drawer of your nightstand. Read one of those."

"A romance novel?" Kate asked, thinking that wasn't at all what she needed to read at the moment, since the only bit of romance she'd ever experienced occurred last night…and would probably never occur again.

"Inspirational romances," Mrs. Tingle said. "The ones where God is in the center, and He makes it last. Those are the best kind, and I think that's what you need to read about, to see

how He can work things out, even when forgiveness has to occur along the way. You aren't
the only one who's ever made a mistake in life,
dear. In fact, the only one who didn't…died because the rest of us do."

Kate blinked, taken aback by the wisdom
spouted from the sweet lady currently stash-
ing her suitcase in the closet. "Thank you," she
said softly, "for your kindness, and for believing that I might have changed."

Mrs. Tingle turned from the closet, walked to
where Kate still sat on the bed and placed her
palm against Kate's cheek. "Oh, honey, you've
got God in you. I can see it. And if you give all
of them time, they'll see it, too. Now you pray,
relax and read. We've got church tonight, and
you need to go."

"Oh, I don't think I can," Kate said, shaking
her head at the very thought of attending the
same church as Mitch.

"Nonsense," Mrs. Tingle said, patting that
hand against her cheek and then turning to
leave. "I don't think you can afford not to. You
can ride with us. We'll leave at 6:45 p.m."

Mitch entered the church parking lot frus-
trated that he found himself searching for
Kate's car.

"Is Miss Kate here?" Dee asked from the backseat.

Emmie had been dozing in her car seat, but she piped up at the mention of Kate's name. "Kay-Kay?"

Odd that just over a week ago they'd never met the lady and now they wanted her to be a part of each day. Mitch knew exactly how they felt, which only made him angrier. How would he explain the fact that they wouldn't see her anymore? And had she, as Mitch suspected, left town? Or would she actually stick around and attempt to see Chad as she'd planned? Did she really think Chad would give her another chance?

He pulled into a parking space next to Bo and Maura's car. They were gathering their Bibles and climbing out, and they wasted no time hurrying over to open Dee's and Emmie's doors. Bo promptly picked Dee up for a hug, and Maura scooped up Emmie and received one of her trademark openmouthed kisses on the cheek.

"You two are a sight for sore eyes," Bo said, putting Dee down and holding her hand as they started toward the building.

"We've missed y'all," Maura said, snuggling Emmie as she carried her along.

Mitch grabbed the diaper bag and Bibles and

followed the group. "They've missed you, too, but I hear you had a good time at the beach."

"Oh, it was wonderful," Maura said, "but it'd have been better if you were there."

"We'll try to go next time," he said, and he meant it. If he'd have gone to the beach with them this year, he wouldn't be experiencing such a hole in his heart from Kate's appearance in his world.

And as soon as he had the thought, L. E. and Annette Tingle's car entered the church parking lot. Mitch automatically lifted his hand to wave, but then he saw the pretty face in the back window looking directly at him…and then looking away.

"Who's that with L.E. and Annette?" Maura asked, and then she gasped. "Mitch, that isn't her, is it? Hannah told us what happened, how she tricked you into hiring her. That's just awful, if you ask me, after what she did to Chad and all."

"Now, Maura, we're walking into the church building. Let's keep our thoughts positive, okay?" Bo gently chided.

"She didn't exactly trick me into hiring her," Mitch said, and then wondered why he felt the need to defend her.

"Sure seemed that way to me. If you'd have

realized who she was, you wouldn't have brought her in your office, and you certainly wouldn't have asked her on a date. Oh, Mitch, I'm so sorry you had to go through that."

The date hadn't been so bad. Not bad at all, in fact. But Mitch knew better than to state that truth, since so much about the past week with Kate had been less truth and more fiction.

"Daddy, it's Miss Kate!" Dee said, turning completely around and using her free hand to wave wildly to the lady walking behind L.E. and Annette. "Can I go see her?"

"Oh, dear," Maura mumbled.

Mitch didn't know how he was going to handle his daughters' adoration of Kate if she continued to stay in Claremont. He'd really thought she would've left town by now, but evidently she was more determined to talk to Chad than he'd realized. How exactly did she plan to support herself in Claremont without a job?

"Kay-Kay!" Emmie said, reaching over Maura's shoulder toward the trio crossing the parking lot.

"I'll drop Emmie off at the nursery," Maura said, picking up her pace. "Bo, you take Dee to hers." She shot another glance back at Kate and gave her a look that should've scared the woman into leaving church, maybe even leaving town.

"Maura, please, settle down," Bo said.

"She has no business here, Bo," she said.

Brother Henry, their preacher, stood at the top of the steps to welcome everyone to the church and apparently heard Maura's comment. "Now, Maura, you know everyone is welcome here, right?"

She visibly swallowed. "Yes, Brother Henry." But she walked even faster as she passed him and made a beeline for the nursery.

"Sorry about that, Mitch. You know how women are when they feel like someone they love has been done wrong. She's concerned about you and the girls, that's all. There's no reason in the world why that young lady can't come to church and worship with all of us if she's feeling it on her heart, and I'll try to talk to Maura more about that when we get home," Bo said.

Mitch nodded. He certainly wasn't feeling as though he should defend Kate's presence at church, but he also didn't want to be standing here in the lobby when she entered. So he walked into the auditorium and took a seat beside Matt and Hannah.

He chatted with both of them but couldn't keep himself from casually scanning the people entering the auditorium. He almost didn't see her, since she slipped in behind a group and quickly took a seat on a back pew by herself. There really wasn't a reason that she couldn't sit with some of the people she'd met around town. She'd gotten to know quite a few over the past week, between their trips to the square and also her phone calls regarding policies. But she obviously wanted to be alone.

Maybe she thought Mitch had told the entire town who she really was, but she should know him better than that. Then again, he thought he knew her better than to think she would have lied to him the entire time she'd been in town. And he'd never have thought her the kind of person who could have left her husband and baby girl behind.

Maura huffed out an exaggerated breath as she plopped down on the other side of Hannah. "It took me a while to drop Emmie off because Annette was running behind, probably because of that person she brought along."

"Who do you mean?" Hannah asked, and then Mitch heard her intake of breath as she spotted Kate on the other side of the building. "Oh, my, Kate's here."

Bo, returning from dropping off Dee at class, sat next to his wife. "I think it's a good thing she's here," he said to Hannah.

Hannah nodded and quickly recovered. "Me, too, Daddy. It's just, well, it's all kind of strange. But I agree that it's good she's in church." She glanced to Mitch. "I'm still sorry I had to be the one to tell you everything."

"I'm glad you did," he said, then turned his attention to the elderly man making the announcements. After he finished, they sang a couple of songs, and Mitch shifted in the seat to glance at the only occupant on that back pew. She looked straight ahead toward the pulpit, never venturing even a passing glance in his direction.

And then Brother Henry took his place in front of the congregation and announced, "Tonight I've decided to put our study of Hebrews on hold while I cover a topic that I believe would be beneficial for all of us this week. Forgiveness and redemption, specifically as displayed in the lives of Joseph, Peter, Paul and the woman at the well."

Mitch didn't know what had prompted Brother Henry to change his topic, but he knew one thing. He'd had his toes stepped on in church before, but he had a feeling this time they were going to be smashed completely.

Kate listened to the preacher describe the terrible things Joseph's brothers had done to him, throwing him in a well to die, telling his father he'd been killed by a wild animal and then selling him into slavery. And yet, when he saw them again, he forgave them, even loved them.

Then Brother Henry talked about Peter, how he was known for his faith…and also his lack of faith, when he started sinking in the water and again when he denied Christ three times. Yet Jesus forgave him, even loved him.

And he discussed Paul and how he'd first been mentioned as a tormentor of early Christians and as the man who held the coats of the men who stoned Stephen. He'd persecuted Christians, and yet Christ knew his repentant heart and forgave him. Loved him.

Kate swallowed thickly and glanced over to the center pews, where Mitch sat with his family. She locked gazes with him and wished she had told him the truth last night. Then, because looking at him and at the hurt on his face pierced her heart, she turned her attention back to the preacher. Why did it feel as if the lesson were aimed directly at her? As if Brother Henry knew how desperately Kate craved forgiveness from those she'd done wrong? From Chad, and now from Mitch.

By the time he started discussing the woman at the well, Kate's tears wouldn't stop falling. In each instance the preacher mentioned, someone had done something wrong, and no little thing. The offenses were terrible. And in each instance, they were forgiven, and they were loved.

Why was he torturing her with this lesson, talking about what she wanted while Kate knew it wasn't possible? Mitch's reaction this morning had verified the fact that even if they were able to forgive, they couldn't forget, and they sure wouldn't give her a second chance. Pretty soon, the whole town would know who she was, and then everyone would behave that way. These people in the pews wouldn't smile at her when she entered the church. They wouldn't speak to her when she met them on the square. She'd simply be the woman who, like Mitch said, abandoned her husband and child and who left anything and everything behind while she satisfied her own desires.

Brother Henry hadn't stopped preaching, but Kate couldn't take any more. Her crying was so steady now that she had to clamp her jaw tight to keep from sobbing aloud, and she didn't want to try to explain to the members of the congregation why the woman on the back row appeared to be at a funeral instead of a Wednesday-night lesson. So she stood, left the auditorium, crossed the empty lobby and headed outside.

She hated that she hadn't driven herself, because if she had she could leave. But she'd let the Tingles convince her to ride with them, so she'd have to wait, since both of them had Wednesday-night duties, Annette with the nursery and her husband teaching a class. So instead of fleeing in her car, she found her way to the darkened playground on one side of the building, sat on one of the swings and waited for the service to end. Maybe she'd spot the Tingles walking out and meet them at their car without even having to speak to another church member.

But, as one of the church doors opened and a sliver of light from the lobby fanned across the ground, Kate knew she wasn't lucky at all. Because she easily recognized the tall, muscular figure also leaving the service early...and walking her way.

Mitch heard every word of Brother Henry's lessons in spite of his awareness of the pretty lady on the back pew...and the fact that she was crying. He saw her trembling throughout the preacher's depiction of Joseph's brothers, Peter's denial and Paul's persecution. But when he'd mentioned the woman at the well, Kate's head had bowed, her tears dripping freely, easily visible from Mitch's vantage.

Those tears pierced his heart, and when he saw her stand and quietly leave the auditorium, he couldn't take any more. He waited for Brother Henry to say a few more words, then he left, too.

Exiting the building, he spotted her, the moonlight catching the pale yellow of her dress as she sat on a swing in the playground. Her shoulders were curved forward, head slightly bowed, and he was pretty sure tears were still falling when she looked up and saw him.

Mitch had no idea what to say, no idea what he was about to do. But he knew without a doubt that what he'd done this morning, blowing up at her and bringing up every sin of her past, wasn't the right thing.

He heard her breath catch as he stopped in front of the swing and looked down to see her eyes swimming in tears, her face and neck damp from the streams.

She ran her palms across her cheeks. "I..." she whispered, her voice sounding scratchy and raw. Then she swallowed and tried again. "I am sorry I came here tonight."

"I'm not."

Her eyes lifted, hands gripped the chains holding the swing in place. "You're...not?"

"No," he said. "I know you needed the lesson tonight, and that's why God has you here." Then he cleared his throat and added the part that hurt most. "But I want you to realize that I needed it, too." When she didn't say anything, he forged on. "I shouldn't have said the things I did this morning, shouldn't have judged you based on your past."

"I should have told you myself," she said.

He nodded. "That would have been better," he said, but even as he said the words he knew the truth. "But then..."

"Then you'd have never hired me, would you? You wouldn't want someone like me, someone who's done what I've done, working for you, or being around Dee and Emmie," she said, her voice still raspy from crying. "And you probably still don't."

He thought about how much pain she'd caused Chad by leaving, and then he thought about how much it would hurt Dee and Emmie if they got too attached and then she did the same thing.

Were they already too attached?

Was he?

Mitch couldn't make any promises about whether he could encourage Kate's relationship with his daughters. He also couldn't make any promises about whether he would trust her enough to have a personal relationship with her himself. Those were things he needed to think about, pray about.

But he knew one area that he could help her with now, and he'd simply start there. If she were going to try to stay in Claremont, talk to Chad and see about having a relationship with Lainey, then she needed a job. And she was a good office manager.

"You left work early," he said, deciding not to respond to the second part of her question about whether or not he'd allow her to be around Dee and Emmie. He'd take this whole forgiving thing one step at a time. "Leaving early without giving me any indication of when you're coming back could cause someone to get fired."

She blinked. "I thought you wanted me to leave," she said. "And not come back."

"Don't you think you should ask your boss about something like that instead of merely making an assumption?" he asked. Before she could answer, he added, "So I can't cut you any more slack. If you're late tomorrow morning, I'll have to fire you. You understand?"

Her eyes fluttered through enough blinks to clear her tears, and she nodded. "Yes, I understand."

Satisfied that he'd done as much as he could do toward forgiveness right now, Mitch turned and walked back into the church.

Chapter Twelve

Mitch stared at his computer screen while Kate rummaged around her desk the way she did every day at noon, neatening her files, logging off the computer, withdrawing her purse from the drawer. Just two days ago, he'd have been standing near her desk and joking with her while she got ready to leave, and then the two of them would head to the diner and chat, maybe even flirt, over their meal.

But today they'd said less than a dozen words to each other since she'd arrived, and now was no exception.

"Do you—" she started, then her face paled when he looked up. "Um, do you want me to get you anything for lunch while I'm out?" she asked.

"I brought something from home."

"Okay." She took a couple of steps and then

stopped as though she were going to ask him something else. Mitch waited for the question, but then she audibly inhaled and exhaled and proceeded out the door.

He listened to her car start and watched through the window as she left, then he made his way to the back, grabbed his lunch and ate the leftover chicken while working at his computer, the same way he'd had his lunch every day...until Kate came to town.

He missed being with her now, but he wasn't ready to say he was okay with what she'd done back then. He was "getting okay," he supposed, coming to terms with the fact that she was the woman whom the entire town had despised merely three years ago.

How would the people of Claremont treat her after Chad got back and the truth came out to everyone? Mrs. Tingle knew and believed Kate deserved a chance to redeem herself; she'd told Mitch as much last night when he'd picked up Emmie from the nursery. And then she'd also added that she was pretty sure Kate had strong feelings toward him, and that she was also pretty sure he had them for her, too.

"Strong feelings" was an understatement, at least on his part, but he wasn't going to admit that to Mrs. Tingle, especially after the day he'd had yesterday with Kate. Even though she'd disappointed him, lied to him, he still couldn't stop thinking about her. And neither could Dee and Emmie. They had asked him multiple times why Kate didn't come over yesterday. He could only imagine what they'd be like this afternoon if they didn't get to see her again.

His cell phone rang, and he saw Maura's name displayed. "Hey, Maura. Everything okay?" She never called him during the middle of the workday unless Bo needed help with something or unless one of them was sick.

"No, Mitch. Everything isn't. Listen, I don't know what's going on, or if RuthEllen Riley got her facts messed up. But I was at the beauty shop this morning getting a trim, and Ruth-Ellen was talking about your new office manager. Saying how nice and helpful she was when RuthEllen called in to pay her bill…this morning."

Mitch should've known this was coming. "Mmm-hmm."

"What does that mean? 'Mmm-hmm'? Are you saying she did talk to Kate today? She didn't have her days mixed up and talk to her last week, before you found out the truth?"

"No, RuthEllen definitely called this morning," he said, recalling hearing Kate's end of the conversation.

"And talked to Kate?"

"Yes, she did." He tapped a few keys on his computer, not because he needed to look something up but mainly because he needed some kind of a distraction while Maura grilled him. The minesweeper game was the first thing that he found, so he clicked the start button, selected a square…and hit a mine.

Not a good sign.

Maura's end of the line grew so silent that Mitch momentarily thought she'd hung up.

"Maura?" he questioned.

"What are you doing, Mitch?" she asked, her voice no longer angry, but confused.

"I'm trying to put Brother Henry's lesson into practice, working on forgiveness."

"But," she said, then whispered, "God, please help us." Then she took a couple of deep breaths and said, "Mitch, do you really think Chad will want her to be in Claremont after what she did? How do you think he's going to feel when he finds out you've given her a job?"

"I don't know, but I do plan to talk to him about it, after he gets back and after Kate's had a chance to talk to him first."

"Well, he's not going to talk to her after what she did. Why would he?"

Mitch could think of one good reason. "Because she's Lainey's mother."

His comment seemed to stump her, and she huffed out a breath. "Can I just tell you the truth, what's really bothering me?" she asked.

"Yes, please," Mitch said, thankful to cut to the chase. "What is it, Maura?"

"I don't think she needs to be around you, not professionally or personally. And I really don't think she needs to be around the girls."

"Why's that?" he asked, closing his eyes and wondering where this conversation was headed.

"Because the girls are already hooked on her, and that doesn't need to get any worse, because she's liable to up and leave again. And, if you want to know the truth, I think you're already hooked on her, too. And I can't stand the thought of her hurting you the way she hurt Chad."

Mitch swallowed and thought about the events of the past two days, particularly when he'd sat at this very desk and screamed at Kate until she'd left the office in tears. "Honestly, Maura, I'm beginning to think she didn't hurt me nearly as much as I hurt her." He saw Kate's car pull into the parking lot. "I've got to go.

Thanks for calling. I'll think about everything you said."

"Please do, Mitch. You know we love you."

"I love you, too," he said, disconnecting as the door opened and the office phone began to ring.

Kate hadn't been able to eat anything more than crackers. She didn't feel well, her stomach in knots, undoubtedly due to the loss of a potential relationship with Mitch…and the impending arrival of Chad and his family to Claremont. She couldn't wait to see Lainey, but in order to see her precious little girl, she'd have to gain Chad's approval.

And now she wasn't certain how to make that happen. Mitch had decided to tolerate her in the office; that was the best way to put it. He'd been cordial and hadn't brought up her past at all today, but he wasn't the guy she'd gotten to know over the past week. Wasn't the guy she'd started to fall for. And even though he tolerated her, had maybe even forgiven her for her past mistakes, he'd still clearly put up a wall between them. They were coworkers now, nothing more, nothing less. No friendly banter between them as they worked. Definitely nothing flirtatious happening, either.

And she missed all of that. She missed Mitch, period. Even though they'd sat in the same room for the majority of the day, she missed him. And she felt achingly alone.

Unlike the earlier part of the day, Mitch actually looked at her as she entered, so Kate held up a hand in a small wave then darted toward the ringing telephone. She dropped her purse and picked up the receiver. "Gillespie Insurance Agency, this is Kate. How can I help you?"

"I didn't believe it."

"Chad," she said.

Mitch looked at her and then stood as though he were leaving. Obviously, he thought she wanted privacy for this conversation. But she didn't want to hide anything else from Mitch, and she'd start that transparency right now.

She cupped a hand over the mouthpiece and whispered, "No, Mitch. Please stay."

He looked confused, but he returned to his seat, while Kate slowly made her way to the chair. *God, please, help me say the right thing.* "Chad, I—I was trying to wait until you got home so I could talk to you in person."

"Hannah texted Jess to let us know you were back and that you were working for Mitch. Seems she didn't want us to end our vacation with the shock of your arrival in town. So I'm asking you to leave, before we get back. There is no reason for you to be in Claremont, and you know it."

"I need to talk to you. About Lainey."

He grumbled something, but Kate couldn't make out the words, and then he said in a hushed tone, as though pushing the words through his teeth, "You lost all rights to talk to me about Lainey three years ago when you walked out that door. Your parental rights were terminated, Kate. You have no reason—no right—to talk to her or see her…or even be around her. Do you understand? Jess is her mother now, and you're not about to come in and confuse Lainey about that. She doesn't even remember you, and I refuse to let you ruin our lives…again."

"Chad, if you would just let me talk to you in person, I have something to tell you. I've changed, Chad, and I hate the person I was back then. But I'm not that way anymore. I've—gone through a lot. And I've turned to God to get me through it." She'd thought she'd cried so much over the past twenty-four hours that she couldn't shed another tear. But she'd thought wrong, because her eyes burned as the tears pushed through. "I've finally found faith."

Another grumble, or growl, echoed through the line. "I'm glad that you think you've got your life on the right track, Kate. Really, I am. Because if anyone ever needed to turn their life around it was you. But that doesn't mean you can come turn our lives upside down, just because you've realized you have a conscience."

"It isn't that, Chad. I don't want to see you only because I'm trying to do the right thing. I want to see you because I want—I need—to see my little girl."

The growling voice returned. "She isn't your little girl, Kate, and she hasn't been for three years. She's ours—mine and Jessica's—legally, and there's nothing you can say or do to change that."

"I'm not trying to take her from you...."

"Good, because it isn't happening. Ever."

"But I have to get to know her, Chad. She doesn't even need to know that I gave birth to her. Just let me be some part of her world." She looked toward Mitch and saw that his mouth had flattened, and his head shook slightly to the side as if he knew there would be no changing Chad's answer.

And there wasn't.

"No." The single word seemed to be his final verdict, and Kate's throat constricted.

She couldn't give up.

"We're coming back into town on Saturday,

and I don't want even the slightest chance of running into you in Claremont. So tell Mitch that you're quitting the job. I get that he didn't know who you were to start with, but I don't understand why in the world he's got you there now that he knows."

"I think he's trying to forgive me," she said softly, and the look in Mitch's eyes said he knew she was talking about him.

"Good for Mitch," Chad said. "And just because I don't want you around Lainey, or around us, that doesn't mean I can't forgive you. I meant what I said. It's great that you've turned your life around. But whether I forgive you or not, that doesn't give you the right to reenter our lives."

"I have to see her," Kate said. "I need to have some semblance of a relationship with my little girl."

"She isn't your little girl!" he repeated, this time bellowing each word into the phone.

"Yes, she is," Kate said, gathering the strength to say everything before she lost her courage… or Chad hung up the phone. "She's my daughter biologically, and there's nothing you can say or do about that!" She hadn't meant to yell, but he wasn't listening to her talk, and if yelling was his method for handling this conversation, then so be it.

"The courts gave her to me," he said, his voice now low and steady. Undeniably angry.

"Let me be a part of her life, Chad. I need that so much. I need her so much. There's no way you can know how much I need her in my life."

"You haven't even called to check on her in three years, Kate. Now you expect me to believe you can't live without having her in your life? Why is that? What changed?"

"I told you, I've changed," she said, her tone shifting from anger to pleading—begging. "And I want to get to know her so badly because…" She really hadn't planned on telling him this over the phone.

"Because why, Kate?"

"Because I *can't* have any more children. Lainey is all I have, all I will *ever* have! Please, Chad, let me see her. Let me get to know her. Let me—let me love her, Chad, and maybe she could even…" Kate sucked in a raspy breath. "Maybe she could even learn to love me? Not as her mommy, but as whatever you want. I could be like aunt. Or just a friend. I don't care what you call me, Chad, but let me have a place in her life. Please, I'm begging you!"

She gripped the receiver and prayed. *Please, please, please. Forgive me. Give me a chance. Please, say yes!*

"No."

Chapter Thirteen

Mitch put the girls to bed and then went out on the porch. Ever since Chad had called his office this afternoon, he hadn't stopped thinking about Kate's side of the conversation. The pain in her voice haunted him, as did the sound of her begging Chad to let her see her daughter.

And the look on her face when his friend told her no.

But Chad's anger was a direct result of the Kate he knew three years ago, not the person she'd become since. Hadn't Mitch also been angry when he realized who she was, what she'd done? But then he had time to think and to realize that she, like everyone else, had made mistakes. She was sorry for those mistakes, and she wanted another chance. Mitch understood that now. He saw it when he looked at her, heard it when she spoke.

He'd sent her home after her conversation with Chad had ended, partly because she was too upset to work and mostly because Mitch didn't know what to say to make her feel better. The one thing she wanted was the chance to be a mother to Lainey, and that was something Chad wasn't allowing. At least not yet. Maybe not ever.

Mitch had texted Chad and received no response. He'd called, and it went straight to voice mail, so he left a brief explanation, saying he hadn't realized Kate was "that" Kate when he'd hired her, and then he also said he wanted to talk to Chad, because he truly believed she'd changed.

Obviously, Chad didn't agree and didn't want to talk to Mitch about it over the phone. Mitch knew his old buddy would come see him personally when he got home so they could discuss what had happened. Chad was a good guy, and they'd been friends since elementary school. He'd forgive Mitch.

But would he forgive Kate?

"I can't *have any more children. Lainey is all I have, all I will* ever *have!"*

Her words, delivered in a panicked cry, had replayed in Mitch's mind all afternoon. No wonder she'd been so eager to help with Dee and

Emmie. More than anything else, Kate wanted to be a mom.

Mitch wondered why she couldn't have more children. Did it have something to do with that doctor's appointment? Because she'd never said that much about it, not the type of appointment it was or what she'd learned from the doctor.

He thought of Lainey, one of Dee's best friends, a beautiful little girl with blond curls, big blue eyes and a smile that always seemed on the verge of laughing. She had Kate's smile, Mitch now realized, and her bright blue eyes. But Kate's hair was inky-black and curly. Chad said she'd been blonde when they dated and married. Why would Kate change her blond locks to black, not that she didn't look beautiful with her ebony hair and ivory skin, but why change? He'd heard that some women changed their hairstyle when they were upset or when they experienced a dramatic life change. Maybe Kate had dyed hers when she realized she'd given up her only child and couldn't have more.

His cell phone rang, and he fished it from his pocket to see Maura's name illuminated on the screen. "Hey, Maura."

"Mitch, I'm afraid I have some bad news."

He'd had plenty of bad news this week, so he figured he could handle a little more. "Okay, shoot."

"Autumn has a fever, and she can't keep any food down. I'm thinking that she caught that same virus Dee and Emmie had last week. I was hoping she would keep from getting it since we were out of town when it hit the majority of the kids, but it got to her after all."

"I hate that for her," he said, remembering how difficult it had been for him and Kate to take care of the girls last week when they were sick. He and Kate, taking care of Dee and Emmie. It'd felt so right, working together to run his business...and his family. She'd blended in as though she belonged here, and for a brief span of time, he'd thought she might.

"I hate it for her, too," Maura said. "I'll take care of her while Hannah has her screening appointment in the morning, but we won't be able to go to Muffins with Mom. I am so sorry."

"It's okay," he said, not wanting her to feel bad when she needed to take care of Autumn. "I'll work something out."

"I was thinking that maybe you could keep them out of the day care tomorrow? Take a day off of work and spend it with them, a daddy-and-daughters day? Undoubtedly they'll be talking a lot about mommies at the day care, since it is Muffins with Mom, and it might just draw attention to the fact that their mommy isn' here. What do you think? Could you take a day off for the girls?"

Mitch knew her well enough to know there was more to her question than she let on. She wanted him to take a day off of work and spend it with the girls not only because the girls didn't have a mother figure for sharing muffins, but also because she didn't want Mitch at work... with Kate. "I shouldn't take off of work tomorrow. I didn't get as much done yesterday or today as I would have liked, and I'll need to catch up."

"Problem with your assistant doing enough work?" she asked.

"She's had a rough couple of days." Mitch set his jaw, then decided to ask the obvious. "Maura, what would it take for you to believe that Kate might have changed? Because the truth is I believe she has."

"You didn't feel that way last night," she reminded him.

"I had to think about it. Pray about it," he said. "So, what would it take?"

"I don't know," she said, her voice losing the steely edge she'd had a moment ago. "I guess I'm scared."

Now they were getting somewhere. "Scared of what?"

"Of the fact that Hannah said you seemed to

be falling for her, and the fact that she's hurt people in the past. I don't want to give her the opportunity to hurt you, or the girls, or…"

"Or what?"

"Or me and Bo," she said. "We see you as a son, and I've prayed that when you found someone again after Jana—and we knew you would, eventually—that she'd be a sweet, kind-hearted God-loving soul who wouldn't want to sever our relationship with you, or with Dee and Emmie."

So *that* was what was going on. Maura was afraid that Mitch would leave them behind if he ever found someone else. And then he'd taken an interest in Kate, and she knew her history, so she panicked.

"Maura, no one—and I mean *no one*—is going to harm our relationship. You're the only family I have, and you're the only grandparents the girls have. I love you, and they love you. No matter who comes into my life, we aren't leaving yours."

She sniffed. "Thank you, Mitch."

"You're welcome. And don't worry. Somehow, everything will be okay."

"I know it will. And I'll start praying about my attitude toward her, but please, promise me that you'll be careful with your heart."

"I'll try."

"And I'm sorry again about Muffins with Mom."

"It's fine. Don't worry at all. Everything will be okay," he consoled her, and then said good-bye and hung up.

"Will everything be okay, Mitch? For me?" Kate's voice, carrying across the porch as she climbed the steps, took him by surprise, but he was glad to hear it. Very glad. He'd wanted to talk to her about her conversation with Chad, but he needed her to decide if and when she was ready to confide.

"I think everything will," he said honestly, then patted the swing beside him. "Want to sit and talk?"

"If you don't mind. I came over because I need someone to talk to. I know Mrs. Tingle is happy to listen, but I—well, I wanted to talk to you."

"I wanted to talk to you, too."

She sat on the swing and that hint of peaches teased his senses. "Really?"

"Really," he said.

"You can go first," she said, her voice trembling as though she were nervous about this conversation.

Mitch didn't want her to be nervous, not

around him. He'd hurt her this week because he'd judged her based on her past. But it wasn't his place to judge. And now he realized how wrong he'd been.

"I wanted you to know that I believe you, that you aren't the same person that Chad knew back then and that you want to start over. And truthfully, I believe you deserve that chance. I can see it in the way you act, the way you talk, but most of all in the way you are with Dee and Emmie." He could still see Dee, snuggled in her bed tonight, clutching her Snow White figurine close, the way she had each night since he'd bought the prized toy. "It's obvious how much you care about them and that you'd never do anything to hurt them."

"You believe that now?"

He nodded. "And I plan to tell Chad that, too, when I see him."

She rubbed her fingertips over her eyes. "I appreciate that, more than you know, but I believe he's made up his mind. I've been praying all afternoon that he will talk to me, listen to me and let me explain what all has happened and how very much I've changed. And I want him to know that I'm not in any way trying to take Lainey from him and Jessica. I wouldn't even have to be 'Mommy,' because I don't want to steal Jessica's role. I just want to be *something* to her."

Mitch nodded and said another prayer that Chad's heart would soften toward his ex. Chad's ex. It was so difficult for Mitch to see her in that light. Because every time he was around her, he still felt a pull toward her himself, and he knew the feeling wasn't one-sided. Right now, he wanted to scoot next to her, wrap an arm around her and take care of her as she went through this pain. But there were obstacles now. His family, for one. His friend, for another. And then, a small amount of fear at what would happen if he surrendered his heart...the biggest obstacle of all. Because if he did, he risked not only hurting himself, but also the girls.

No, he should stay on this side of the swing.

"Mitch," she whispered.

"Yeah?"

"Would you—hold me?"

So much for staying on his side of the swing. Chad had hurt her terribly today when he said no; Mitch wouldn't—couldn't—do the same. Besides, he wanted to hold her probably as much as or more than she needed to be held.

He edged toward her, wrapped an arm around her and pulled her close. She seemed even smaller, even more fragile, against his side, and he wanted to protect her from all of the pain absorbing her world. He leaned his head against hers and whispered, "I'm sorry I hurt you, Kate."

"I'm so sorry I hurt you," she said, placing one hand on his chest and then looking up at him, her lips so close that if he edged forward they would touch.

He didn't need to go there. She said she wanted to talk, and Mitch still needed to find out the rest of the story. "Kate, today, when you talked to Chad, you said that you couldn't have any more children."

Her shoulders trembled, and she shook her head. "I can't, and that's what makes it even worse that I left Lainey back then. I gave her up, and now I can't have more children."

"What happened?" He rubbed a hand up and down her arm as he continued holding her, comforting her, wanting to help her through this difficult conversation.

"A year and a half ago I started feeling bad, lots of little problems that turned into bigger problems. It started with pain in my back and lower abdomen. I ignored it for a while, and that was a mistake," she said, her voice becoming clearer as she spoke. "You should never ignore pain."

Mitch's stomach knotted. He had a feeling he

knew where this conversation was headed because he'd had a similar one with Jana a couple of years ago, when she'd blamed herself for
not going to the doctor quickly enough the first
time the cancer hit.

*Don't let her say it, Lord. Please. I can't take
that again. You know I can't.*

She cleared her throat and continued, "And
then, by the time I went to the doctor, I'd waited
too long."

Mitch closed his eyes, tried to keep his pulse
steady, get the tension ratcheting in his body
under control so she couldn't tell how badly
he didn't want her to say...what he knew was
coming.

"It was ovarian cancer, and they had to work
fast to try to remove it because I'd waited too
long. And then I started the chemo and radiation." She lifted her hand to her hair. "I'd always
been a blonde, but when my hair came back,
this is what I got."

He nodded, unable to speak. Jana's hair had
come back a lighter shade of brown than before and a little more curly...the first time. And
the second time, when the cancer returned,
she hadn't lost her hair because she'd opted
against treatment, not wanting to hurt the baby
she carried.

And then after Emmie came, there wasn't time for treatment, and he lost his wife.

"I'm in remission now," she said. "And if this week's screening comes back clear, I can start going every six months to the doctor instead of every three." She looked up at Mitch, and he forced his jaw to relax. "But I can't have children anymore. The cancer took that away from me."

And cancer had taken Jana away from Mitch. "I'm sorry, Kate."

"That's why I want so much to be a part of Lainey's world. For a while there, I thought I might never get to see her. I didn't know if I would make it. But I did, and I believe God let me survive because He wanted me to have this chance to know her. But I need Chad to say yes."

"I'll talk to him and see if I can help," Mitch said, lifting his arm from around her and easing away from her on the seat. His subtle way to end the conversation and to give him a chance to get away.

She took the hint and stood, wrapped her arms around her waist and said, "I appreciate that so much." She stayed there for a moment as if expecting Mitch to stand up and hug her goodbye, which would be the normal way for this visit on the porch to end, if not with a kiss, but Mitch didn't budge from his position on the swing.

"Good night, Mitch."

"Good night, Kate," he said, then watched her walk away while he processed everything he'd learned. Kate was a cancer survivor. So was Jana, right up until the cancer came back. He'd barely made it through that horrible time and wouldn't have wanted to continue living if it hadn't been for Dee and Emmie. He never wanted to go through that kind of pain and worry again, and he certainly didn't want to put his girls through it. Therefore, he couldn't get any closer to Kate. He'd help her try to work things out with Chad, and he could even be her employer. But Mitch had been stung by that disease one too many times, and he wouldn't risk losing someone else he loved to it again.

Which meant one thing. He couldn't let himself love Kate.

Chapter Fourteen

"I forgot my backpack, Daddy."

"Okay," Mitch said, turning to unlock the door and then waiting while Dee darted inside. Emmie, taking her time to get fully awake this morning, laid her head on his shoulder while they waited on Dee.

"Got it!" Dee said, grinning as she ran toward the door.

Mitch was running behind getting them to the day care, and he wondered if that was God's way of telling him that he shouldn't try to be the only daddy at Muffins with Mom. They could go in late, after the morning breakfast, and maybe they'd forget that today was the special day.

Then again, this was Dee, who never forgot any type of special occasion. And she proved that with her next question.

"Is Aunt Hannah going to want a blueberry muffin or a strawberry one?" she asked, jumping off the last step and then skipping toward their car.

"Aunt Hannah had to go to the doctor this morning, so she can't come after all," Mitch said, wishing he'd have explained the change of events before now.

"Is GiGi going?" she asked. Apparently she knew the typical requirement for this event was a mommy, or at least a female. Maybe they should stay home.

"GiGi is having to take care of Autumn, because she's sick."

"Sick?" Emmie asked.

"Yes, she's sick," Mitch said, but Dee had stopped a few feet shy of the car.

"Who's gonna eat muffins with us? Last time Aunt Hannah did."

Mitch hadn't thought she'd have remembered the activity from last May, since she'd been only two and a half, but she did. "I know, but this time, Daddy wants to go."

"Daddies don't go," Dee said. "It's mommies and grandmommies."

At least she added the grandmother part. Perhaps some of the working moms sent a grandmother to fill their spot. That would eliminate his little girls from being the only ones without a mommy present. But that didn't fix the fact that they'd probably be the only ones there with no female whatsoever. He thought about taking them to the diner instead. "Why don't we do something different today and go to Mr. Tolleson's place for breakfast?"

Dee planted her feet. "You said we could have muffins with everybody at school."

"Okay," he said, opening the car door and hoping—praying—that she'd climb in. "Let's go, and we will."

"Not you. It's not the daddy day. It's the mommy day. But we don't have a mommy so we need Aunt Hannah or GiGi."

He felt as if she'd kicked him. *We don't have a mommy.* And he didn't know how to fix this morning's problem.

"Kay-Kay!" Emmie chanted, reaching over his shoulder.

Mitch turned to see Kate exiting the B and B and looking their way.

"Miss Kate! She could go with us!" Dee said, and before Mitch could stop her, she yelled, "Hey! Miss Kate! Can you go to school with us?"

Kate's head tilted in question. She crossed the

street with her long emerald-green dress drawing attention to her petite figure as she moved.

Mitch's heart thudded in his chest. She had no idea how beautiful she was, smiling at his children.

"Can you have muffins with us?" Dee asked. "Pleeeeease?"

"Muffins?" Kate asked, looking from Dee to Mitch.

"Today is Muffins with—" he started, then didn't know whether he should phrase the morning event differently, but Dee plowed ahead.

"It's Muffins with Mom day," she said, "but our mommy is in heaven, so we bring someone else, but Daddy shouldn't come, 'cause he's a boy and it's for girls. The daddy one is another day."

Kate looked from Dee to Mitch and then back to Dee. "Well, I'm not sure…" She glanced back to Mitch, and he saw more than a question of whether she could go to the breakfast with his girls. He saw the question of whether he trusted her with Dee and Emmie, and he saw more— the question of whether she would be a good mommy if she ever got the chance.

"Please?" Dee repeated, reaching for Kate's hand. "Please, Miss Kate?"

"Kay-Kay?" Emmie said, following her big sister's lead.

Mitch knew he couldn't deny her this, or deny his girls. "It'd mean a lot to them, and to me, if you'd go have muffins at the school this morning. You can come to the office after the breakfast ends."

Kate's smile burst forth, lighting up her face. "I'd love that, Mitch. Thank you so much."

"Yay! Miss Kate's going!" Dee cheered, letting go of Kate's hand and hurrying toward the car. "Come on, Daddy. We don't want to be late!"

He smiled and worked hard to keep that lock intact on his heart. This was to help Kate and his girls. It didn't mean he was somehow putting Kate into the female role in Dee's and Emmie's lives for good—or in his, for that matter.

Kate parked her car and entered the day care with Mitch, Dee and Emmie, still shocked that he was allowing her to spend the morning with the girls this way. This was what a real mother would do, and she was elated. It also said that he trusted her with his girls again. Another reason for elation.

Maybe this was a sign of things to come. Maybe Chad would give her another chance, too.

Please, God.

"Come on, Miss Kate, and I'll show you where my class is," Dee said, taking her hand as soon as she exited the car and pulling her toward the yellow building. Other moms were walking in with their children, all of them smiling and some chatting about the muffins.

Kate couldn't wait.

Mitch opened the door for them and then told the lady in the office that Kate would be sharing breakfast with the girls. Then he helped get Kate signed in before walking with her to put Emmie's diaper bag in her classroom.

"Daddy, almost everybody is already down there," Dee said, peering down the hall toward the small lunch area. "We gotta go."

"Okay," Mitch said, grinning. "I get the hint." Then he stepped toward Kate and held Emmie out for her to take. "Here you go. Emmie, try not to be too messy with those muffins." His hands and forearms rubbed against Kate's as they transferred his little lady, and Kate easily remembered his arm around her last night. However, she'd noticed that at some point in their conversation he'd gradually pulled away.

That was okay. She knew this would take time, earning Mitch's trust again, maybe even earning the chance at him "falling for her," as he'd said the other day, again. She could be patient. He was worth the wait.

And today they were making progress. He was letting her take the girls to Muffins with Mom. No, she wasn't their mom, but even the semblance of being in that position gave Kate chills. She could be a good mommy. She *would* be a good mommy...if Chad would let her.

"'Bye, Daddy. Love you!" Dee said, continuing down the hall.

"Wuv you," Emmie said.

Mitch smiled. "Love y'all, too." Then to Kate, he said, "I'll see you at the office."

She nodded. "I'll be there. And, Mitch?"

He stopped walking. "Yeah?"

"Thanks."

He nodded, turned and continued out the door.

"Come on," Dee said, ushering her down the hall and toward the room filled with tiny tables, smiling women, chattering children, lots of sippy cups and an abundance of muffins.

Kate figured if she could paint her own picture of heaven, this might be it. Well, if she could add a daddy to her picture. And if he happened to be Mitch.

But she'd take this one step at a time.

"Hey, would you like to sit with us?" one

young mother called, and Kate nodded, then sat with a new friend, laughed with Dee and Emmie and felt as though her world might actually start becoming okay.

By the time they finished breakfast and Kate took Dee and Emmie to their respective classrooms, she couldn't stop smiling. This was one of the best days of her life, and it wasn't even nine o'clock yet.

Then, as she started to leave the building, a lady with auburn hair pulled into a high ponytail stopped her in the hall. "You're Kate, right?"

Kate was certain she hadn't met this lady before, but maybe she'd spoken with her on the phone. Or talked to her at church. She was trying to learn all of the names and faces at the church. "Yes. Have we met?"

"No," the lady said. "But I have heard a lot about you, and I guess I wanted to say hello and that, well, I hope everything works out okay."

Kate swallowed. "You've heard a lot about me?"

"Yes. I didn't realize you were coming to Muffins with Mom. Normally we have it the Friday before Mother's Day, but we had so many kids out that week with that horrible virus that we postponed it, and then after one classroom got over being sick, the next one would get it.

I'm just glad we were able to have it in May," she said with a grin. "In June we'll need to have Doughnuts with Dad, for Father's Day." The woman pointed to the next classroom door. "My name is Angie. I help teach the four-year-olds' class here," she said. "Dee will move into our class in the fall."

"Okay," Kate said, still not understanding why that meant the lady had heard a lot about her.

"My co-teacher is Jessica Martin."

And then the other shoe fell. Kate bit her lower lip. She knew Jessica was with Chad now and they were still on vacation. Chad had said they weren't returning until tomorrow. But this lady had already heard a lot about Kate? Of course she had. Naturally Jessica would have talked about the woman her husband had been married to, the one who'd tried to abort their baby, cheated on him and then lied to him about Lainey being his. What wife wouldn't talk about an ex who was that evil?

Kate felt the muffins churning in her belly. "I've changed," Kate said simply. "I have."

"And I believe that people can," Angie said. "But Jessica called me last night to see how things were going in the class while she's been away, and she also needed someone to talk to about learning that you were back and working with Mitch. We've grown very close teaching the class together."

Kate nodded. "I'm not trying to hurt her," she said. "I just want to have a place in Lainey's life, if they'll let me."

"And that's the reason I wanted to talk to you. Jessica is scared that you're going to try to take Lainey away, and since Chad isn't her biological father, I'm guessing you would have some kind of a chance."

"I don't want to do that. That isn't why I'm here, to take them to court. I wouldn't put them—or Lainey—through that. It wouldn't be right, because I gave her up. But I'm hoping that they will still find it in their hearts to give me another chance to at least know her."

"And I want you to know that I'm praying that they do, and I told Jessica last night that I felt they should let you at least see her again." She glanced over her shoulder and saw that they were the only two in the hall. "Most everyone here knows, because I don't try to hide it. I made the decision, after all. But I also gave up a child. My son. I put him up for adoption when I was sixteen because I wasn't ready to become a mother. And I have no idea where he is now. I've tried to find him, but I haven't had any success. I wouldn't want to ruin his life and his family situation, but I'd just like to see him. I think it'd give me peace of mind, you know. And I am hoping that you'll get that chance, too." Her eyes were glistening, and she glanced up to the ceiling to apparently regain control. "Jessica and Chad are good people. And I know they'll make the best decision for their family and for Lainey specifically. But for your sake, I pray that they let you see your little girl."

Her words were a balm to Kate's soul. This woman, whom she had just met, was praying for her to see Lainey. "Thank you, Angie."

The sound of a toppled chair and a loud "Uh-oh!" echoed from the room nearby, and Angie grinned. "Duty calls. You have a blessed day, Kate."

"I will," Kate said, and she prayed she would.

Mitch recognized the older-model silver BMW as soon as it parked outside his office. But he'd thought he would have another day to prepare for his friend's arrival. The front door opened and the owner of the vehicle stepped inside.

"Chad. I thought you weren't coming back until tomorrow."

He closed the door, glanced at Kate's empty

desk and then moved to Mitch's guest chair and had a seat. "I wasn't," he said. "But that's the thing about vacations…you want to enjoy yourself. Jess and I couldn't concentrate on anything but making sure Kate left town, and finally we decided the best thing to do would be to come back early and make certain she did before we ran into her with Lainey." He shook his head. "I don't get it, Mitch. I mean, I understand how you hired her before you realized who she was, but you know now. Why keep her working for you?" He took another glance at the opposite desk. "Or did you let her go?"

"No, I didn't let her go," he said, and didn't divulge that Kate was currently enjoying muffins with Dee and Emmie at the very day care that Lainey attended and Jessica taught. He sure hoped Jess didn't go into work this morning. "Where's Jessica?"

"Home with Nathan and Lainey. And she plans to stay there until I make sure Kate's gone for good."

"I honestly think you should hear her out, Chad. She's gone through a lot in the past three years, and she says that she has changed."

"She *says* she's changed. Do you know how many things she *said* to me when we were married that all turned out to be well-orchestrated lies? She's a master at it, Mitch, and you need to understand that." Chad squinted at him while shaking his head. "Don't tell me you've fallen for her, too."

When Mitch didn't respond, Chad said, "Don't, Mitch. She'll ruin you, and she'll hurt your girls. I can promise you that. Kate only cares about one thing, and that's Kate."

The door shut with a snap, and Kate said, "That's not true."

Chad whirled in the chair and stared at her, shock apparent on his face. "Kate?" Then he shook his head. "What…happened?"

Mitch hadn't thought about the fact that Chad hadn't seen her since she left three years ago. Obviously he'd expected to see the blonde, athletic woman who'd been a sprinter in high school and had a zest for life and adventure that he hadn't been able to contain. He wasn't prepared to see the thin, dark-haired Snow White figure that entered the office.

Kate's face fell, her eyes blinked a couple of times like they did before she cried, but then she seemed to gather her composure and answered, "I have—or, *had*—cancer. But I'm better now. I'm in remission."

Mitch had tried not to think about Kate having cancer, because it made him sick to his stomach to think he was falling for another woman who could be taken from him so quickly. But it also hurt to think about not surrendering to the pull of Kate on his heart. He looked at her, and he saw she no longer looked at Chad, but at him, her eyes so sad that Mitch wanted to tell her that everything would be okay.

But he didn't want to lie.

Kate took the few steps to her desk and leaned against the front as though she were suddenly too weary to stand. She looked even more frail as she faced her ex-husband, the man who had the power to let her see her daughter...or keep them apart forever.

"I've changed, Chad. I came close to dying. I know I did. But I fought to live. Do you know why?"

He shook his head, but he also looked as though he didn't care. "No, Kate, I don't."

"Because I hated everything I'd done wrong, and I wanted a chance to fix my mistakes. I prayed to God to give me that chance, to live long enough to correct my past and to give me the chance to be a part of Lainey's life."

"Like I told you yesterday, I am totally fine with you finding your faith. I'm glad you have. But you can start your new life somewhere else, and you should. This would only hurt Lainey, confuse her, and I'm not letting you do it. I'm asking you to leave town."

"I need to see her, Chad," Kate continued. "You don't have to even tell her who I am. I can just be someone she knows. I don't care. But she's the only child I'll ever have. Please don't keep her from me completely."

"You did that yourself when you left. It's too late for you to start over. Now you can leave town...or we will."

Mitch couldn't believe what Chad was saying, and obviously neither could Kate.

"Wh-what?"

"I've been offered positions at two other campuses. I never thought I'd want to leave Claremont, but I refuse to stay here if you've decided to call this your home. You'll hurt my family, and you'll hurt my little girl."

"I wouldn't," Kate said.

"And I don't believe that." He shrugged. "Your track record isn't that great, Kate." Then he started for the door. "Tomorrow. Leave by tomorrow, before we have the unfortunate opportunity to run into you anywhere around town. And if you don't, then I'm putting my resignation in at the college. It's as easy as that. Your decision. You stay, and we'll go." He slammed the door, stormed to his car and peeled out of the parking lot.

Kate watched him leave, her hand covering her mouth in disbelief. Then she turned toward Mitch, studied him and looked even more... hurt. "I saw the way you looked at me a moment ago. It's the cancer, isn't it?" she whispered.

He'd expected her to say something about Chad, so her comment threw him. "What?"

"I sensed it last night, when we were on the porch. One minute you were starting to feel something for me again, and then you pulled away. I kept trying to figure out what it was, what had happened, and then a moment ago, I saw it on your face. When I told Chad about the cancer, you looked like it hurt you for me to even mention it. And it does, doesn't it?"

Mitch nodded. "It's an awful disease," he said, and hoped that would satisfy her question.

It didn't.

"But that isn't why you pulled away last night, and that isn't why you looked at me that way just now," she said, shaking her head as she spoke. "You can't handle that again, can you? You can't handle the thought of being...close...to someone who's had cancer. So you won't let yourself get any closer to me, will you?"

Mitch couldn't deny the truth. "I'm going to

keep talking to Chad and try to convince him to let you have a relationship with Lainey. I do believe you've changed, and I think if you give him time, he'll believe it, too."

"No, I don't think he will. He said he's leaving town if I stay. You know Chad. He doesn't make idle threats. That night he told me he was quitting med school because I was so unhappy, I thought he was lying, trying to make me feel bad for being so miserable. Then he quit the next day. If he said he'll leave, he'll leave. If I stay in Claremont, he'll go because of what I've done in the past. And you're not going to have anything to do with me personally because you're afraid of what's happened in your past." She took a gulp of air, then turned and opened the door. "I give up, Mitch. I can't win."

Then she left the office, while Mitch hurried to follow her. He cleared the doorway as she opened her car door. "Wait!" he yelled.

She stopped. "Why, Mitch?"

He wanted to tell her because he loved her, or because he believed they were meant to meet, meant to be together and raise Dee and Emmie together. But then the fear of loving her—and losing her—stopped each word in his throat. *Cancer,* his mind whispered, and he saw Jana dying all over again. He wouldn't risk that with Kate.

"That's what I thought," she said, climbing in the car and driving away.

Kate sped away from the office, her foot pressing on the accelerator as Mitch's silence pressed on her heart. He was willing to help her with Chad, but he wasn't willing to give her a chance at himself. And Chad wasn't willing to give her anything toward seeing Lainey. His promise to leave town if she stayed wasn't an idle threat, and that hurt almost as much as Mitch's refusal to let her have a place in his life.

No place in Mitch's life.

No place in Lainey's life.

She'd prayed for God to help her, but everything had only managed to get worse. *Why, God? Why?*

Kate thought about one of the verses she'd leaned on when she was going through the cancer. She couldn't remember the chapter and verse, but she remembered the gist of the message. God wouldn't give her more than she could bear, and if He gave her something to bear, then He would also give her a way to get through it.

"How much more do you think I can bear, Lord?" she cried aloud, as she pulled her car in at the B and B and turned off the engine. Then her phone rang, and she got her answer.

She recognized the number on the display, dropped her head back and cried. "I don't understand, God. Help me understand."

"We won't call unless we need to see you again," the nurse had said when Kate left the doctor's office on Tuesday. And now the doctor's name and number stared back at her from the screen. Kate had no choice but to answer. "Hello."

"Ms. Wydell," the woman said on the other end, "I'm sorry to have to call you with this before the weekend, but Dr. Ayers wanted to get in touch with you today because we'd like for you to come back in on Monday. Hold on and I'll connect you with the doctor."

Kate closed her eyes and listened as Dr. Ayers came on the line. Then she had the conversation she'd never wanted to have again, listening to him explain what would begin again on Monday morning. The cancer was back. The treatments would start over. More chemo. More radiation. More…unbearable life.

Unbearable.

You said You wouldn't give me more than

I can bear. She told the doctor she'd be there Monday morning and then ended the call. *You...lied.*

Chapter Fifteen

Kate sat in her car and waited in the same parking space she'd been in two weeks ago when she found Mitch's job in the classifieds. She'd packed all of her things last night and taken the suitcases to her car before dawn this morning to keep from waking the Tingles. And to keep from saying goodbye.

She hated the way she left, but she couldn't risk Mrs. Tingle convincing her to stay. Staying was no longer an option.

This morning, she'd driven past each place that she'd come to love over the past two weeks. The diner where she and Mitch had shared lunch. The day care where she'd had her first—and only—Muffins with Mom. She could still hear Dee's and Emmie's sweet voices chatting with her as they shared breakfast, still felt the surge of love toward the two little girls who'd so touched her heart…and the abundance of love for the man who'd stolen it completely.

Mitch. How she wished that she could have seen him one more time, said goodbye with a hug. Or a kiss. She touched her lips, remembered being in his arms and experiencing the tenderness of his kiss. She'd never felt more treasured, more loved.

But he couldn't handle even the possibility that the cancer would return. How ironic, that the day he decided it might come back…she'd learned it had.

A few families were gathered in different areas of the park, some picnicking and some practicing baseball on the fields. The wind wasn't conducive to kite flying, so there weren't any of the diamond-shaped images in the sky, but Kate still pictured a pink smiley soaring above the trees…and the feel of Mitch's arms around her when she'd lost control of that kite.

Was that the way the rest of her life would be? Thinking about each moment with Mitch and regretting that they couldn't last forever?

Probably so. But, if it was any consolation, the "rest of her life" wouldn't last that long.

She saw the silver BMW crest the hill that led into the park. Chad still drove the same car he'd driven when they were together, which didn't surprise her. Doctor or not, he wasn't one to be showy about his possessions. He'd been different from her that way, too, because back then, she'd spend their very last dime to make sure she wore whatever blended with the doctors' wives.

How foolish she'd been.

As they'd agreed, Chad parked a short distance away from Kate, and she watched, mesmerized, as the family got out. Chad exited first and was quickly followed by a sandy-haired boy—Nathan, Kate realized. Chad's son with Jessica would be about nine now, which coincided to the size and build of the boy grabbing a baseball bat and ball from the trunk and then running toward one of the fields.

Kate had never seen Jessica, and when she got out of the car and smiled toward Kate, she knew why she'd so captivated Chad in high school. She was naturally beautiful, with flowing brunette hair, an athletic build and a genuine smile. Kate was shocked that she was smiling at her, especially since she knew who Kate was and how she'd treated Chad.

"I'll be right there," Chad called to Nathan, and then he started walking toward Kate's car, while Jessica opened the other back door and helped Lainey climb out.

Kate held her breath, looking past Chad to see the tiny blonde smile up at Jessica and then hug her around the waist.

"Let's feed the ducks, Mommy," she said, reaching into the car to grab a bag of bread.

Jessica shot a glance at Kate and Chad and gave Kate yet another smile, but this one seemed to hold a hint of pity toward Kate. And Kate understood why. Lainey had confirmed what Kate already knew. Jessica was the only mommy that little girl had ever had, and would ever have.

"You can thank Jess for this," Chad said as he neared her. "I didn't want to agree to your 'deal,' but she's got a soft heart, and she finds it a little easier to forgive than I do."

"I'll thank her," Kate said, a lump lodging in her throat at the reality of what was about to happen. She was going to actually meet her little girl.

"And you're leaving town after this, right? That's all you want, to meet her today, and then we don't have to deal with any of this again, right?" he asked.

"Deal with me again, you mean," she said.

He nodded.

"That's the deal," she whispered.

"Okay, then, come on, and I'll introduce you

to my little girl," he said. Then he clarified, "Your little girl, too."

"Thank you for that." She walked beside him toward Jessica and Lainey, who was opening the bread bag and tearing the loaf into pieces beside the pond, while the ducks started swimming toward the prospective meal.

"Lainey," Chad said, when they neared the pair, "I have someone for you to meet."

She squinted as she looked toward the sun to see Kate, and Kate was treated to eyes the exact same shade and shape as her own. "Hey!" she said, grinning with a full baby-teeth smile.

"Lainey," Jessica said gently, "this is…Miss Kate."

"Hi, Miss Kate," she said. "Are you gonna feed the ducks with us? We got lots of bread. I can share with you if you don't have any."

Kate's heart melted, and she looked to Chad, who nodded.

"Go ahead," he said.

"Thank you," she whispered, and lowered to her knees beside her little girl. Then she looked up to Jessica, who was crying, and said, "Thank you so much."

"You're welcome," she said.

"Here you go." Lainey took a piece of bread and handed it to Kate. "But you can't give it to them like that, or they might get choked, so you have to break it up. Want me to help you break it?"

"Yes, that would be very nice." And suddenly, Lainey's small hands were working with Kate's to break the bread and feed the ducks.

"Miss Kate? Why are you crying?" Lainey asked, and then she looked at Jessica and said, "Mommy, are you okay? You're crying, too."

"These are happy tears," Kate quickly said. "I'm just so—so very happy to meet you and feed the ducks."

Lainey giggled. "Me, too!"

With Chad and Jessica nearby, Kate spent an entire hour talking with her little girl and feeding the ducks at the pond. Lainey loved to talk, and she told Kate all about their vacation, how they'd spent a few days at a beach and then some days camping in the mountains and then they'd gone to a big amusement park and ridden all of the rides. She was so excited, so happy, and Kate thanked God for that. And she thanked Him for giving her this hour with her little girl.

When the time was over and Chad and Jessica got ready to leave, Kate prepared to tell her little girl goodbye, but she couldn't make herself say the word. So she stood and watched the family pack their things to go, with Lainey smiling at her before she headed to the car.

Jessica stopped her before she climbed in, and then Lainey, still smiling, ran back to Kate. "'Bye, Miss Kate," she said, and she stretched her arms wide for a hug.

Kate lifted her in her arms. She'd held Lainey as a baby, and she'd hated it, had thought she must not have a single motherly bone in her body, because she'd felt nothing.

But Kate's heart had opened since then, and now she was filled with a warmth and a love so all-consuming that she never wanted to let the little girl go. "Oh, Lainey, I so enjoyed meeting you."

Lainey laughed. "Me, too!"

Kate squeezed her once more, focused on remembering everything about this hug and then put her little girl down and watched her leave.

Chapter Sixteen

"I brought my insurance payment for ya," Chad said, entering Mitch's office and plopping into his guest chair without the anger he'd had a few days ago. He tossed the envelope toward Mitch and then looked at the empty desk on the other side of the room, giving Mitch an indication of the real reason for this visit.

Mitch had been staring at that desk all morning, when he wasn't calling Kate's number and leaving her messages or texting her and asking if she was okay…while wishing he hadn't been an idiot and that she was here, with him, where he believed she belonged.

"Your payment isn't due for two weeks and you always mail it in," Mitch said. "Why don't we talk about why you're really here?"

Chad frowned, glancing at the desk again. "You heard from her?"

"No. Like I told you at church yesterday, according to Mr. and Mrs. Tingle, Kate was gone when they woke up Saturday morning. I've been calling, but she hasn't returned any of my calls."

He nodded. "Yeah, well, I figured if she had wanted you to know about Saturday morning, she'd have told you, so I didn't say anything to you yesterday. But Jess and I were talking last night, and we both think we made a mistake in trying to keep her from Lainey. And after seeing them together on Saturday, we realized that Kate wouldn't do anything to jeopardize our relationship with Lainey and that she honestly just wants to have some part in her life." He shrugged. "But I've texted Kate, too, and she doesn't answer."

Mitch leaned forward in his chair and asked, "What do you mean 'after seeing them together on Saturday'? Kate saw Lainey?"

Chad nodded. "She called us early Saturday morning and offered us a compromise. She said if we'd let her see Lainey, just meet her once, then she'd leave town for good and wouldn't interfere in our lives anymore." He frowned. "I didn't even want to give her that, but Jess said it was the right thing to do, so we did. Met her at the park and let her spend some time with Lainey, feeding the ducks."

Mitch could only imagine how much that meant to Kate, and he wished he could have witnessed the moment when she was reunited with her little girl. "And then she left?"

"Yeah, and promised we wouldn't hear from her again." He shook his head as he looked at Kate's desk. "Now I'm thinking I may have acted too harshly, and now no one can get in touch with her. Jess thought maybe you could ask her to give us a call when you hear from her, and we can work something out about her seeing Lainey some." He lifted his shoulders. "Jess said she believes it's the right thing to do. She reminded me of when she left town when she was pregnant with Nathan and then told me how badly it would have hurt her if I hadn't forgiven her when she came back." Chad looked back to Mitch. "I'm a little slow on the forgiving thing. I tend to hold a grudge for a while first. I did that with Jess, and now I'm doing it again with Kate. But with Kate, I may have lost the opportunity to tell her. So if you talk to her, ask her to call us, okay?"

"She doesn't want to talk to me, either," Mitch said, feeling sick. For all he knew, Kate had changed her number to keep from hearing from any of them. And he had no idea where she'd gone.

"You love her," Chad said, stating a fact rather than asking a question.

"Yeah, I do, but I hurt her Friday, too. Basically I told her I couldn't risk loving someone who might be taken from me again, taken from the girls again." Mitch had mentally kicked himself repeatedly for his fear and for the fact that he hadn't told Kate that he loved her.

Chad winced. "Hey, I can see that. After everything you went through with Jana, watching her suffer and then losing her…you've gotta be scared of that happening again. But if you love her, would you rather go without having her your entire life than having the chance to love her even if it's only for a little while? Plus she's in remission. She could be cancer-free from now on."

Mitch heaved a sigh. He'd been thinking the same thing all weekend. He only wished he'd have thought that through before she left town. "I was stupid."

Chad started to say something but stopped when the office phone rang.

Mitch picked up the receiver. "Gillespie Insurance Agency."

"Oh, yes, hello. This is Patricia Owen with the Winship Institute in Atlanta. I'm trying to reach Kate Wydell. The first contact number seems to be a cell phone that isn't working or is disconnected, and this was her second point of contact. Would she happen to be there?"

"No, she isn't here," Mitch said.

"Dr. Ayers asked me to call and find out if she is running late or if we need to reschedule her treatment. Do you happen to know if she is on her way? She was due in at six o'clock this morning, four hours ago."

"She was supposed to be there at six o'clock?" Mitch asked, his mind rattled from the surplus of information he'd received...and everything else he wanted to know.

"Yes, and Dr. Ayers wants to get her in as soon as possible, so please let her know that we'll put her down for the same time Wednesday morning, and I will continue trying to reach her at the other number she provided."

"I'll...let her know," Mitch said, hanging up the phone and immediately bringing up a search engine on his computer while Chad looked at the screen to see what he was typing.

"What's up?" Chad asked.

"That was a doctor's office in Atlanta," Mitch said, watching the results of his internet search for Winship Institute fill the screen. He clicked on the main website and saw exactly what he feared. "A cancer institute."

"Aw, man," Chad said.

"Her cancer is back," Mitch said. "She had her appointment last week, and she'd hoped it'd come back clear. She told me so the other night. They wouldn't have her come back in unless something was wrong." Mitch stared at the screen, scanning the information about the institute's ability to treat all cancer types. "I let her go because I thought I couldn't deal with the possibility of her cancer coming back. And now it has." He wanted to throw something, kick something. Mainly himself. "But…"

"But what?" Chad asked.

"But now all I can do is think about her, dealing with this alone, and I want to be with her. That's what I should have told her, that if something like that happened, I'd help her through. But I didn't. And now I can't get her to return my calls."

"She isn't returning mine, either. And apparently, she isn't taking calls from the cancer center," Chad said.

Mitch got a sick feeling about that. "Why would she have missed her first appointment?" He remembered how important those appointments were from when he went with Jana. Radiation to shrink the cancer, followed by chemo. The quicker Kate started getting treatments, the better chance for the doctors to remove all of the cancer.

Chad frowned, and Mitch thought he knew why.

"You think she decided not to get treated, don't you?" Mitch asked.

"I don't know. The old Kate would fight tooth and nail to live. She loved life too much to give up."

"But the new Kate?" Mitch asked, knowing the answer.

Chad shrugged as if he didn't want to say it, so Mitch did.

"She wouldn't see a reason to fight to live if she couldn't have a life with Lainey," Mitch said.

"Or, I'm guessing, a life with you."

Mitch shut down the computer and grabbed his keys. "I've got to find her."

"Where are you going to look?"

"I don't know." Mitch felt defeated.

Chad stood and joined him to leave the office. "I'm pretty sure I know a way that you could find her without having to look. You can get her to come to you."

"I'm listening."

Kate walked steadily along the shore, the sand comforting her feet with every step and gently pressing between her toes while the cool water lapped over her ankles. She thought of Lainey, excitedly describing her trip to the beach, and she prayed that her little girl would have many more happy trips to the beach in her life.

The wind carried the salty scent of the ocean, and Kate thought that this might be what heaven felt like, smelled like.

And then she recalled having Lainey in her arms, and sharing muffins with Dee and Emmie, and Kate knew that heaven, for her, would feel like that, smell like that.

She blinked through another batch of tears, surprised that she still had any to shed. And then she silently scolded herself for being so sad. Over the past two weeks, God had given her so much. She'd learned how it felt to truly be in love, because she had no doubt that she loved Mitch, and she always would. And she'd learned the joy of being a mother.

Maybe God let her have so much so quickly because He knew this was her last chance to experience it. She'd been angry at Him a few days ago, believed that He was giving her too much to bear. But she was wrong. She'd dealt with the truth, that the cancer had returned, and she'd found peace, thanks to her time with Mitch and his girls and then her morning with Lainey.

She didn't want to go through those horrid treatments alone, so she'd skip them entirely and enjoy her last days seeing the beauty of God's world before she saw the astounding beauty of heaven.

It would have been wonderful to have spent more time with Mitch, would've fulfilled her every dream to have been a permanent part of Lainey's world. But she'd come to terms with her limitations, and instead of lamenting over what might have been, she decided to reflect on the sweet memories she'd made in the past two weeks.

She picked up a seashell and tossed it into the ocean, then watched it slowly sink through the water to find its new resting place in the sand. Her father had brought her to this beach on Tybee Island when she was five, only a couple of years older than Lainey was now. He and her mother had divorced, her mom leaving with her boyfriend and content to let him have custody of Kate. Kate had been thrilled to stay with her dad. Her mother had never wanted her, and even a five-year-old could recognize the intense dislike she'd had toward Kate. But her father had loved Kate and wanted her to be happy, so when her mother left, they came here and walked the beach.

Then six months later, he met her stepmom, and she had loathed the little girl who always seemed to be in the way. Her hatred for Kate was even more than that of Kate's mother. And her daddy had wanted to please his new wife so desperately that he ignored his daughter completely.

But this beach had created the happiest memory Kate had from growing up, and she wanted to experience that once more…before she saw her daddy again in heaven.

By the time she'd walked the entire stretch of sand and then returned to her car, daylight had shifted to twilight, and a chilly breeze had her holding her arms around herself to stay warm. She opened her car door, sat in the driver's seat and rubbed her feet together to remove the sand. Then she decided that she wouldn't mind bringing a bit of this sand along to whatever destination she chose next, and she swiveled in the seat to put her sandy feet into the car.

She stared at the ocean long enough that the sky deepened from blue to black and the moon peeked out from the clouds. She counted the waves one by one as they fought their way toward the shore, occasional white crests capturing the moonlight, and she became so relaxed, so content, that she closed her eyes. The wind whistled through the tall sea grass, and she almost allowed herself to go to sleep, but then she thought about Mitch, and she glanced at her cell phone in the center of the passenger seat.

She'd turned it off because she knew the doctor's office would call, and she'd left it off all day while she traveled because she didn't want to be tempted to call him and see how he was handling the office without her help, or whether Dee and Emmie had asked about her, or if Chad had mentioned her visit with Lainey.

She reached for the phone and turned it on.

It buzzed to life, text message after text message beeping through at record speed, as well as several voice mails. Kate had expected the doctor's office to call, had known they would, but who were all of these messages from? She couldn't deny that her heart hoped…

Sure enough, Mitch's name scrolled rapidly up her screen. And every now and then, in the midst of Mitch's, would be one from Chad.

She scanned the messages and saw that each one from Mitch was identical, the same sentence sent over and over.

Dee and Emmie need you.

And interspersed between Mitch's messages were Chad's, also identical and repetitious.

Lainey needs you.

Kate responded to one of Mitch's texts.

What's wrong with Dee and Emmie?

And then immediately responded to one of Chad's.

What's wrong with Lainey?

She gave them a full minute to respond, and when they didn't, she dialed Mitch's number.

His voice mail picked up, and she left a message. "Mitch, what's wrong with Dee and Emmie? Call me."

Then she hung up and dialed Chad. And after three rings, she got his voice mail, too. "Chad, this is Kate. What's wrong with Lainey? Call me please."

Had all of the girls gotten sick? Or had something else happened? Was there an accident at the day care?

She brought up the internet on her phone, searched for news stories on the Claremont Day Care.

Nothing.

She cranked the car and then sent another text, this one to both Mitch and Chad.

I'm on my way.

She'd been tired a moment ago, but her adrenaline had kicked in now. It was 9:00 p.m., and she was seven hours from Claremont. She could be there by morning.

* * *

Mitch's eyes hurt from staring down Maple Street and watching for Kate's car. He'd had more cups of coffee than he'd ever had in his life. Maybe that was why his hand trembled as he held the cup. Or maybe it was because he was scared.

His phone rang, and he quickly pulled it from his pocket, saw Chad's name and answered. "Hey."

"Well, how did it go?"

"She isn't here yet."

A pause sounded from the other end of the line. "She said she was on her way. I'm sure she'll show up soon." But his tone said he wasn't so sure.

Neither was Mitch.

"What if something happened? We don't even know where she went or how far away she was when she finally got our messages." He shook his head. "I should have answered her last night."

"Then she'd have asked what was wrong with the girls, and you'd have had to say nothing. And then she might not have come back at all," Chad said.

"She *hasn't* come back at all," Mitch reminded him.

"She will," Chad said, sounding a little more certain. "So, did Lainey do okay spending the night?"

"Yeah, the girls are all still sleeping. Thanks for letting her stay over. I thought it'd be good for her to be here when Kate comes back, but I also thought she'd have gotten here by now."

"No worries. Nathan was already spending the night with Kaden, and Lainey was feeling a little left out, so this worked out fine. And give Kate time. She'll get there," Chad said. "Jess and I are on our way over. We'll wait with you."

"You don't have to do that," Mitch said.

"Yeah, we do, because we're part of why she left, and we want to make sure she knows we've had a change of heart," Chad said. He continued, but with his mouth obviously away from the mouthpiece, "Isn't that the way you put it, Jess?"

"Yes," she answered.

"See," Chad said, "that's the way it is."

Mitch was thrilled that they'd finally seen the "new" Kate and had forgiven her; he only hoped she'd come back so they could tell her. "Okay, I'll see you when you get here." He disconnected and then saw L. E. and Annette Tingle walk out onto their front porch.

"Kate make it back?" L.E. called.

Mitch shook his head. "Not yet." He could see Annette's look of worry even from across the street, then she turned and darted back into her house with her husband following. Mitch had talked to the pair last night about what was going on and asked them to pray for Kate to make it back and to be healthy again. He knew they'd prayed and were probably still praying right now. Mitch had prayed all night, but he wouldn't stop.

God, please, give me another chance with Kate.

The morning sunlight pushed between the rows of cherry trees lining Maple Street and reflected off the hood of a car heading his way. Mitch squinted as the vehicle neared and he stood up when he realized that his prayers had been answered.

By the time she parked the car in his driveway, he was there, opening her door...and waiting to pull her into his arms.

Kate had been upset that she hadn't been able to drive through the night, but when she'd hit Atlanta, she simply hadn't been able to hold her eyes open and had stopped at a rest area to sleep for a while in the car. But she was here, finally. And in Mitch's arms...finally.

"I'm sorry it took me so long to get here," she said. "Are they okay? What happened? What's wrong with the girls?"

He held her so tightly that she felt his throat pulse with his swallow, and then he kissed her hair, and Kate prayed that everything was okay with Dee, Emmie and Lainey.

"Mitch, please, tell me."

"Kate, they're fine. I'm sorry you were worried. All of the girls are fine."

His words shocked her, and she leaned back to look at him, then saw that he was crying. "Mitch? I thought…"

"I'm sorry to get you here this way, but if I told you that Chad and I needed to talk to you, well, you might not have come back. But I didn't lie, and neither did Chad. Dee, Emmie and Lainey all need you. And so do I."

He slid a hand down his face to wipe away the tears, then smiled and brushed a soft kiss across her forehead. "I was a fool for thinking I could live without you. I can't, and I don't ever want to again."

"But, Mitch, wait," she said, hating what she had to tell him, but he deserved to know. "Please, don't say anything else. You wouldn't want to be with me now. I've got…a lot going on…and I can't put you through—"

He shook his head. "No, you wait," he said, giving her another of those smiles that sent a shiver down her spine. "I know. I know what you're going through, and what you're about to go through. I know about the appointment at the Winship Institute."

She blinked. How did he know? "I didn't go," she said. "And I've decided—" she swallowed "—I've decided I'm not going through it again because…"

"Because why, Kate?"

"Because I've done everything I wanted to do, and I don't want to go through that again alone." She shook her head. "I can't."

"That's what I'm saying, Kate. You *won't* be alone. I'll be with you."

Her mind reeled. "You said you couldn't handle that again. I know I didn't misunderstand. That's what you said, and I can't ask you to."

"You're not asking," he said. "And I'm not, either. I'm telling you that I'm going through it with you. I'll take you to the treatments. I'll take care of you on the rough days. And I'll celebrate with you on the good days. And when it's over, and the cancer is gone, we'll have the biggest party this town has ever seen."

Kate couldn't believe what he was saying. He

knew what those treatments were like. She'd be sick, constantly. She'd get even thinner because she wouldn't be able to eat. She'd lose her hair again. "I can't let you do that." She shook her head so much that she felt light-headed. "I won't."

"But you see, that's part of the deal," he said, his voice so smooth and steady, as though he had no uncertainty in his offer at all. And Kate couldn't fathom why. He'd been through this before with Jana. He should turn and run the other way knowing what he would potentially go through again. But he didn't. Instead, he pulled her closer, his arms caressing her trembling frame as he said the words that Kate had longed to hear. "I love you, Kate, and there's nothing you can do to change that. And I'll love you completely, through sickness and in health, if you'll say yes."

Kate's mouth fell open, and she stood wide-eyed as he eased away from her and then lowered one knee to the ground. "Mitch, what—what are you doing?"

He withdrew a small box from his pocket. "I bought this yesterday, and then I prayed all through the night that God would give me the chance to give it to you…if you'll say yes."

"It's going to get rough," she whispered,

her words pushing through the thickness in her throat.

"I know," he said, still holding the box toward Kate.

"I'm going to look terrible. Awful," she continued.

"Not to me."

Kate wasn't so sure, but his eyes said he believed it. And they also said so much more. He loved her. Mitch truly loved her.

"Kate, do you love me?"

Her heart soared. "Yes."

His smile stretched wide. "Then marry me."

"Hey, how long are you going to make him kneel there before you give him an answer?" Chad asked.

Kate turned to see him standing with Jessica beside his car, parked at the street. And another car was pulling in behind him, and yet another behind that. Bo and Maura climbed out of the second car, and Matt, Hannah and Autumn got out of the third. And then she saw L. E. and Annette Tingle had walked across the street, Mrs. Tingle's arms holding a large dish, and everyone seemed also to be waiting on her answer to Mitch's question.

She turned back to the guy still looking up at her with hope—and love—in his eyes.

"Say yes, Kate."

She nodded. "Yes."

He put the ring on her finger so quickly she hardly felt it glide on, then before Kate had a chance to speak, he'd stood and scooped her into his arms. "You've just made me the happiest man," he said.

"I hope you'll still say that next month, when we finish radiation and head into chemo," she said.

He laughed. "In sickness and in health, as long as we both shall live, and I'm going to pray for God to make that a very, very long time. We've got a lot of living to do."

Her tears were instant, and her hopes were enormous. "I'm going to pray for the same thing."

"Everyone," he said, "I'd like to introduce you to my fiancée!"

Kate was shocked at the excited cheers and laughter from the group. Undeniable happiness, even from Chad, who shouldn't be happy at all that she was marrying Mitch and staying in Claremont. But he sure looked happy. Then he and Jessica walked over, and Mitch finally placed Kate back on the ground.

"Listen, several people here want to talk to you, and it isn't only about wishing us well," he said with a wink. "So while I go in to check on the sleeping princesses, I'll give them a chance to talk…and to congratulate you, because this is an amazing day." He turned and punched Chad in the arm. "I'm getting married."

Chad laughed. "So I hear." Then he and Jessica looked at each other and then at Kate.

"We were wrong," Jessica said, "to say you couldn't have some place in Lainey's life. That isn't at all what true forgiveness is, and we're sorry."

"We want you in Lainey's life," Chad added. "At this point, we think it'd only confuse her to try to explain that you're her biological mom, but we'd like you to still be a part of her life. She's mentioned Miss Kate a few times over the past couple of days, so I believe you've already made an impression."

"She has?" Kate asked, happiness filling her soul.

They both nodded.

"And eventually, when we think she's old enough to understand, we'll tell her, but until then, we'd like for her to know Miss Kate," Chad said.

"Thank you," she said. "Thank you so much."

And then she found herself being hugged by Chad and Jessica, something she'd never imagined happening, and it felt so good to be accepted. Forgiven.

Then Bo, Maura, Matt, Hannah and Autumn walked up behind Chad and Jessica. "Can we talk to her for a second, Chad?" Bo asked.

"Sure." Chad gave Kate a smile, wrapped an arm around his wife and then started toward Mitch's porch.

"We wanted to tell you," Bo started, but Maura shook her head and cleared her throat.

"No, Bo," she said. "This is all my fault, so let me do it."

He smiled at her. "Okay."

"I've done a terrible job at following what Brother Henry preaches, and what the Bible says about forgiving and not judging, and all of that. Last night, when Annette called the prayer line and asked all of us to pray for your safety, I was miserable."

Mrs. Tingle, hearing her name, stepped forward and lifted the gigantic dish in her arms. "I wanted everyone to pray, and those prayers worked," she said happily. "Which is a good thing, since I made a huge breakfast casserole. I need all of these folks to help eat it!"

Her comment, delivered as she and L.E. walked past the group and toward the house, broke the tension for a moment, but Maura wasn't done speaking yet.

"When I heard Annette's message on the prayer line, I started praying to God right then and there to forgive me and to give me a chance to tell you how sorry I am for treating you badly."

"You didn't—" Kate interrupted, but Maura wouldn't have any part of it.

"Yes, I did. Maybe not directly, but indirectly for sure, because I told Mitch he shouldn't give you another chance, and I was wrong. So now I'm asking if you'll forgive me."

"Of course I do," Kate said.

"And there's something else," Maura continued. "In our eyes, Mitch is our son. He's family. And I want you to know that in becoming a part of Mitch's family, well, you'll become a part of our family, too, if you want." Her voice caught on the last few words, and she waved a hand in front of her face as though the emotions were getting the best of her.

Bo and Hannah both stepped beside her and wrapped arms around her, and Bo said, "We've lost a daughter. We'll never have Jana back, not until we see her again in heaven. But we feel blessed that God is giving us the opportunity to have another daughter—" he looked to Hannah "—and a sister in our lives, if you'll have us."

Kate's happiness bubbled over, her tears spilling down her cheeks as she stepped toward the group. "You don't know how much that would mean to me," she whispered, "to be a part of a real family."

"Kay-Kay!"

Kate turned to see Emmie toddling onto the porch with Dee and Lainey close behind, all of them still in pajamas. Emmie clutched her bulldog in one hand and her nighty-night blanket in the other, Dee had her Snow White and Lainey held a stuffed teddy bear.

"Miss Kate!" Dee said, with equal excitement.

"Hey, Miss Kate!" Lainey said.

The trio grinned at her, with Dee and Lainey hurrying down the steps to give her hugs and Emmie standing on the porch with her arms wide and waiting.

Kate hugged Dee and Lainey, laughing through the tears that she simply couldn't control. And then Mitch picked up Emmie and brought her to join in on the group hug.

"Daddy said you went away 'cause you were sad," Dee said. "Are you still sad?"

"No," Kate said, hugging them all as she spoke, "I'm not sad anymore. In fact, I'm very, very happy."

"We're glad you're happy," Lainey said, her

pretty face lighting up with her smile. "It feels good to be happy."

"Yes, it does."

Chad stepped out onto the porch, looked at the group and nodded his approval. "Jess was right. This is the way it should be."

"I couldn't agree more," Mitch said.

"So, girls, y'all ready for breakfast?" Chad asked. "Mrs. Tingle has your plates ready."

"Okay, Daddy," Lainey said, turning to start up the stairs with Dee following. Then she stopped at the top and looked back toward the people still standing in the yard. "Miss Kate, are you going to have breakfast, too?"

Kate swallowed then nodded. "Yes, Lainey. Thank you for asking. I'll be right there."

Lainey smiled and ran through the doorway with Dee.

"Eat?" Emmie asked, as Mitch scooped her up.

"Yes, sweetie, you've got a plate, too." He grinned at Kate. "You ready to go in?"

She tried to say yes, but instead a whimper escaped, and her tears turned into a steady flow. "I'm—sorry. I'm—just so happy." She swiped at her wet cheeks. "You know, me being real emotional, that's part of it, what we'll go through over the next few months. I'll cry a lot."

"Well, if I do my job, I'm guessing you'll laugh a lot, too," he said.

And just like that, her smile pushed free. Mitch could make her laugh. In fact, he not only made her laugh, but he made her love…and he made her want very much to live.

Epilogue

As far back as anyone could remember, there had been weddings at Hydrangea Park, but there'd never been a wedding on a T-ball field… until today.

The entire town helped haul the bleachers from all of the surrounding fields to this one, so that even the outfield had a grandstand. And by the time the wedding started, every seat was filled and people even stood against the fence, all of Claremont eager and excited to see Mitch Gillespie find happiness again.

Kate wore a long dress, white satin with a lace overlay. It wasn't a bridal gown, per se, but it was perfect for this casual—and quite beautiful—setting. Maribeth Walton, the owner of Consigning Women on the square, had helped Kate find the vintage gown.

Mitch wore a tan suit and a blue tie that

brought out the brilliant blue of his eyes. Kate focused on those eyes as she walked toward the center of the field, where Brother Henry waited with her groom.

As they'd requested, the ceremony was short, with the preacher reading the passage of love from First Corinthians 13 and then having them repeat the standard vows.

Kate's hair had come back pitch-black and curly after her chemo had ended, just like last time. It was still short, a little past her ears, but growing fairly quickly. Mitch said he actually liked it short, because it made it easier for him to kiss her neck. And he kissed her neck quite often, because he said he liked the way it made Kate laugh.

Mitch had kept her laughing over the past year. Through the radiation and then the chemo, he'd found a way to make her smile, even through the days when she felt so weak and tired that all she wanted to do was cry.

She loved him even more for that.

And then, when they learned that the treatments had worked and that the cancer was gone, they hadn't stopped laughing, smiling…living.

Their time together revolved around each other and also around the girls. All of the girls. Dee, Emmie…and Lainey. Kate was thrilled to see them all huddled together and clapping as she and Mitch completed their vows.

"They're beautiful," she whispered.

"Yes, they are," he said, cupping her face within his hands and rendering her speechless with his love. "And so are you, Mrs. Gillespie."

Kate really liked the sound of that.

Brother Henry cleared his throat and announced, "I present to you Mr. and Mrs. Mitch Gillespie."

The crowd cheered so loudly that his next words were drowned out by the sound. So, as soon as they could hear each other again, Mitch turned and asked, "Preacher, can I kiss my bride?"

Brother Henry's laugh echoed through the microphone pinned to his lapel. "By all means."

Their kiss received another deafening round of applause, as well as some resounding "ewwwws" from the kids in the dugouts. And then the preacher gave his final announcement.

"As all of you know, the reception will be held at the big pavilion over by the picnic areas after the game. So I guess the next order of business is…" He shrugged, cleared his throat and yelled, "Play ball!"

The four-and five-year-olds who'd been waiting semi-patiently stormed the field, while the guests all laughed and the bride and groom moved to their "honorary seats," satin-covered chairs in the dugout for Lainey and Dee's team.

Kate had never been to a T-ball game before, and she hadn't wanted to miss their first one just because it was the same day that she and Mitch had planned their wedding, so they'd moved the wedding here. And it couldn't have been more perfect.

She and Mitch laughed as they helped each little girl or boy get their batting gear on and head out to the plate, and then they cheered on both teams as they played five innings where everyone got a turn to bat, no one got out and no one kept score.

She didn't know when she'd had more fun.

And when the game ended, her groom carried her over the threshold of the dugout and then all the way to the picnic area, where they joined the families of Claremont and became the family of Kate's dreams.

* * * * *

Dear Reader,

I knew from the moment I introduced you to Kate as the villain in *Her Valentine Family* that I eventually wanted you to see her redemption story. We've all done things we wish we could change in the past. Obviously, Kate's mistakes were huge, but nothing too huge to warrant God's forgiveness. However, gaining forgiveness from those she'd wronged was another story, as it often is in life.

Whether you're the one wanting forgiveness or the one needing to grant it, I hope Kate and Mitch's story will help you see its healing power, both for the one who has offended another and for the one pardoning their sin.

I enjoy mixing facts and fiction in my novels, and you'll learn about some of the truths hidden within the story on my website, www.reneeandrews.com. If you have prayer requests, there's a place to let me know on my site. I'll lift your request up to the Lord in prayer. I love to hear from readers, so please write to me at renee@reneeandrews.com. Find me on Facebook at www.Facebook.com/AuthorRenee-

Andrews. And follow me on Twitter at www. Twitter.com/ReneeAndrews.

Blessings in Christ,

Renee Andrews

Questions for Discussion

1. Kate started out as the villain in *Her Valentine Family,* but now she has become the heroine. Is it possible for someone to go through that drastic of a change in real life? Do you know of any examples, or has this happened to you?

2. How difficult do you think it was for Kate to return to Claremont?

3. In many cases, women who give up their children for adoption do not know anything about the whereabouts of their children after their parental rights are terminated. Do you see this as positive or negative?

4. Do you think Kate's inability to have more children affected her intense desire to see her daughter, or do you think she'd have wanted to see Lainey either way?

5. How do you think Chad's wife, Jessica, initially felt when she heard Kate was back in town?

6. Have you ever held on to a grudge, even nurtured it to make it stronger instead of

finding the ability to forgive the one who has done you wrong? Are you still growing your grudge, and if you are, do you think it would give you peace to let it go? Can you? And if you can't, what would it take for you to do so?

7. When I wrote the scene where Kate saw Lainey, I found myself crying. Did that scene hit you that way? Why, or why not?

8. Mitch had lost his first wife to cancer, and he had a fear of having a relationship with Kate when he learned she'd had the same disease. How difficult do you think it'd be to put yourself in the same position to lose the one you love again?

9. How did Mitch's faith factor into his ability to have this new relationship with Kate?

10. How did Kate's history with her own family initially affect her ability to have a healthy relationship?

11. Although Maura fought Mitch's relationship with Kate at the beginning, she eventually forgives her and then asks forgiveness

from Kate. Why did Maura need forgiveness? What did she do wrong?

12. How important do you think it was to Kate to have Bo and Maura tell her she would now be a part of their family? Why?

13. Lainey isn't going to know that Kate is her biological mother until Chad and Jessica believe she is ready to learn the news. Do you agree with this?

14. How do you believe Lainey will handle the truth when she learns that Kate is her biological mother…and that Chad isn't her biological father? Or, if you were Chad and Jessica, would you ever tell her? Why, or why not?

15. What was your favorite scene in the book? Why?